Zoom Theater 2020

A collection of new plays performed by friends.

By Rick Regan

<u>Players:</u>

Ed Backes

Celia Gannon

Chris Gannon

Jean Claire Glanville

BT McNicholl

Lyn Peticolas

Rick Regan

Maura Vincent

Zoom Theater 2020

A collection of new plays performed by friends

ISBN: 9798564560931

Printed in USA

Published by Lights Go Inc

PO Box 40039

Raleigh, NC 27629-0039 USA

First printing, 2020

This book is dedicated to my lovely wife, Ann Gleason, who has encouraged me to keep working, keep writing and to produce this book. Thank you, dear. /Rick

Contents

Introduction

This book is a gathering of friends, both the characters who show up and the actors who bring these characters to life.

We (mostly) all participated in the student theater group, CenterStage, at the Catholic University of America in Washington, DC in the mid-1980s. Today those days seem a long time ago, but the Covid-19 pandemic has changed the way many of us spend our days, in particular quarantining for most of 2020. So, given the chance to team up on Zoom calls, we decided to make our weekly group not just a reunion but also a functioning theater group again.

Now I certainly don't have any illusions that our performances will be the Toast of The Post, as admittance is limited to our gang and not critics or even an audience, but our weekly gatherings have provided a safe and comfortable space to gather, check in with each other and then perform some short piece. I am humbled and incredibly grateful to have this talented team, and who are willing to wrestle many of my silly stories into something close to real live theater.

The pieces included in this collection are not the only ones that we have read during the summer and fall, now becoming winter. Ed Backes has had several original pieces. Chris Gannon has a full length screenplay, now optioning for a motion picture. JC Marshall has entertained us with some original *dream pieces*. Lyn Peticolas, our ever-faithful Zoom-host, shared an essay from an education periodical, which while not drama was extraordinary in her thoughtful and gracious insight into education policy and the grass-roots experience of teaching. Maura Vincent let us glimpse at a one-woman show she is working on, and we expect front row seats when we are back to some normal times. And BT McNicholl, ever the Broadway scion, brought us a revival of a George M. Cohan show, or rather a premier, as it had never been produced. I have not included these items for this collection as they belong to the people involved and will be best served in their own spotlight.

The characters in these stories range from a Greek goddess, to airline pilots, to medieval knights and kings, to Marty, the talking mule, and many others. The stories typically deal with characters trying to get to the center of a question, and wondering about the consequences on their lives when or if they find the answers.

For example, in *Way of the Iguana*, the son Luis considers the life of his mother, a poor peasant in Mexico, and says to his girlfriend, "She was a saint, but she wanted to be a martyr. She wanted to suffer, for God." Here he is, staring into the question about his own direction in life and his own meaning in life, and reflects on his mother's piety. Does he pity her? Does he envy her devotion? You can decide.

In *Tears into Wine*, the goddess Aphrodite appears in the kitchen of a modern-day woman with a desperately ill husband. Her sister doubts that the goddess can help but Aphrodite comments, "So many prayers, but so little faith… You have prayed and I am here." Of course Agatha, the sister, does not expect salvation to appear, literally in front of her, in the form of a 10,00 year old Greek goddess. But then, who would?

In *Sword in the Stone*, the First Minister faces the dual betrayal of his loyalty to both his wife and his king. What is a man to do when his understanding of his life evaporates in lies? Hmmm…

Cal's Dream Show may seem an odd addition to these mostly closed-loop dramas, that is they are generally self-contained worlds, but this piece is a response to BT McNicoll's revival of the Cohan script of *Musical Comedy Man*, which is entertaining, puzzling and mildly frustrating. I wrote an alternate version where the story is closer to my preferred style of linear drama. But of course, with so many of my stories, there is usually a place where the slight-of-hand business starts and things get a bit off the rails, like when Willie, a chicken-factory ice hauler, shows up for dinner with Alan Greenspan, in *Win a Dinner with Alan Greenspan!*

In this year of pandemic, quarantine & lockdown, a presidential election and so much more, we have tried to keep connections, make some Zoom theater and have some fun. I am deeply indebted in gratitude to all the actors and friends of our group.

<u>Zoom Theater 2020</u>:

(in first-name alpha order)

- Celia Gannon, Kansas City, MO
- JC Marshall, Briar Cliff Manor, NY
- Lyn Peticolas, El Paso, TX
- Maura Vincent, Hollywood, CA

- BT McNicholl, Los Angeles, CA
- Chris Gannon, Kansas City, MO
- Ed Backes, New York City, NY
- Rick Regan, Raleigh, NC

And for my other readers and reviewers, I am so grateful for your attention and feedback. Thank you.

Here is hoping that 2021 is fair weather and clear sailing for all of us.

/Rick Regan, Raleigh, NC, November 9, 2020

Cal's Dream Show!

By Rick Regan, July 15, 2020

This is the story of an old vaudeville and Broadway showman. He lives in an assisted-living home now but dreams of doing one more big show.

Characters:

Cal	Vaudeville & Broadway entertainer, retired
Grace	Granddaughter of Cal
Naomi	Nurse and aide to Cal
Stan	Cal's old friend and entertaining partner
Helen	Cal's wife, deceased
Solly	Broadway dancer
Bella Abzug	women's rights activist from the 1970s
Will Rogers	entertainer from the early 20th century
William Sullivan	Grace's fiancé

Players:

Cal	BT McNicholl
Grace	JC Marshall
Naomi	Lyn Peiticolas
Stan	Rick Regan
Helen	Maura Vincent
Solly	Ed Backes

SCENE: Setting is a simply furnished apartment. There is a door on the back wall. The door is reality and people who come and go through the door are real. In the dream people enter and exit stage left and right because they are memories or imagined people.

Cal is sitting in a chair in an apartment. His head is nodded forward, and he is asleep.

Naomi, the in-home attendant is around 50 years old, wearing a nurse-type outfit.

She comes in, sees Cal asleep and moves around quietly, so as not to wake him. She picks up a stray coffee cup, folds a newspaper and generally straightens up. Seeing Cal still sleeping, she goes to another chair and sits down. She closes her eyes and rests, possibly sleeping lightly.

The scene is of this older couple: he nearly 80, famous and wealthy enough to have in-home staff, and she around 50, getting up early to take a bus to take care of this old man. But here they are, a couple sharing naps in an apartment together.

There is a knock at the door and Naomi wakes, goes to the door and is handed a food delivery bag.

She sets it on the table, gets plates and utensils ready for Cal's lunch.

She wakes him for lunch. Maybe rolls over a tray with a bowl of soup with noodles. He eats some.

Knock at the door. Granddaughter Grace comes in. She is probably 25 or so.

GRACE: Hey, Grandpa Cal! How are you today? I wanted to come by and see what you have been up to.

CAL: Oh Grace! How wonderful to see you. Have you had lunch? Would you like some soup?

GRACE: No, but thanks. I can't stay long but I wanted to see you.

NAOMI: How are you, Miss Grace? Good to see you.

GRACE: Thank you, Naomi. I know you are taking good care of my Grandpa Cal.

NAOMI: Oh, he's an easy one.

CAL: Grace, how about this? A dear friend of mine from Broadway came by this morning and said she's got a new script for me. She's got a show going up and needs some 'heavy weight' talent for the marquee to fill the seats.

           Looks like I start rehearsals in two weeks. How about that?

GRACE: (looks at Naomi, puzzled)

NAOMI: (looks at Grace, shakes her head, indicates that Cal is making it up)

GRACE: Uh, well... gosh Grandpa, that sounds great. Congratulations. I can't wait to hear all about it when you get it going.

CAL: Oh it's going to be like old times: Dancing, singing, full orchestra, the whole business!

GRACE: OK, Grandpa. OK. Sounds like fun.

CAL: We'll give the people what they really want: Entertainment. That's the thing!

GRACE: Listen, Grandpa, I have to go now, but I will come back later. I have a surprise for you!

CAL: What is it? What is it?!

GRACE: I can't spoil the surprise! I'll see you later. (Kisses him and Exits through the door.)

CAL: Well how about that? Isn't she great? She's great.

NAOMI: Oh, she's lovely Mr. Cal. (Naomi takes the lunch things away, goes to the sink to clean up)

CAL: That was tasty. Thank you, Naomi.

(He takes up the newspaper on his lap and reads briefly)

NAOMI: (after cleaning up she goes to a chair at the edge of the stage)

Mr. Cal, I'm going to take a quick rest. You let me know if you need anything.

CAL: Mmm-hmmm. OK.

NAOMI: (closes her eyes and drifts off to sleep)

CAL: (droops the paper on his lap, tilts his head back and goes to sleep also. Both are sleeping.)

[Knock at the door]

CAL: (stands up smoothly and strides towards the door but does not open it)

STAN: (Stan, the old writing partner, enters from one side of the stage)

CAL: (moving easily, as if he is a much younger man, greets Stan)

Stan! How are you? I haven't seen you in an age.

STAN: Hey, Cal! How have you been?

CAL: You know you're just in time. I've got an idea for a new show and I'm glad you are here.

 We can kick it around. Like old times!

(Cal swings the chair around and they both sit)

STAN: Say, Cal do you remember that gig in Nashville, maybe in Sixty-Five?

 Oh, it was a while ago. Who was the conductor for that show? Do you remember?

CAL: Nashville, eh? Sure, that was Ol' Charlie, Charlie Pantone.

 We called him Charlie Pantomime because he waved his arms around and moved his whole body back and forth when he had the stick. Yeah, haven't thought of him in years, Ol' Charlie Pantomime!

STAN: That's it. That's the guy. He always had the dames all over him at the party after the show. That guy could really swing!

CAL: (laughing) Oh man, he could swing! Ol' Charlie...

STAN: What was the name of that doll he always asked for, the dancer, tall, good looking gal. Sheryl?

CAL: That was Helen. You know I married her. We were together for a lot of great years.

STAN: Oh, yeah, yeah. I remember her. She was great. She was good for you, Cal.

 She was in your rodeo show, "OH- HI OH!". Remember that one?

 At the party after the opening, Ol' Charlie ordered Kansas City chops for the whole table, with pitchers of gin Martini's to go around. He was a laugh riot.

CAL: One of a kind.

 But listen you remember Joan Riddell, from LA? We did a song and dance thing for her, a run at the Palace. You remember her?

STAN: Sure, sure. Smart lady. She still around?

CAL: Still around? She was sitting right where you are sitting now, just yesterday.

STAN: No!

CAL: Of course! She's got a new play. She wants me for it, a serious bit.

STAN: No music? No dance? That's what people come to see. Hear you sing and see you dance.

CAL: Hey, I still got it, you know.

> (to orchestra conductor – note: there is no real orchestra or conductor)

> > Say, Charlie! Give me a little something to work with.

> (Cal gets up gracefully, and begins a smooth soft-shoe dance as the music comes in. He moves around the apartment with ease and style. Song ends.)

STAN: Looking good, Cal. You got all the moves.

CAL: I want to give people what they really want. I don't want to do some mopey play about sad people. I want to really get 'em! Girls, dancing! Guys, singing! That's the stuff. Real entertainment.

STAN: Who's going to be the boy and the girl, the Love Interest? You gotta have a love interest.

CAL: I'd love to work with Helen again. Is she available? I want her in that really great Vegas Showgirl get up, with feathers in the tall hat. The whole thing!

> (Helen enters from the side, wearing a fabulous Showgirl outfit.)

> (She is around 30, a healthy, attractive woman. She strides in and greets Cal and Stan.)

HELEN: Hi-ya Cal! Hello Stan! Great to see you guys!

CAL: Hey there, beautiful!

HELEN: So what are we working on? Got a cracker-jack number for me?

STAN: Sure doll! Give a swing around to this new one.

> (to the imagined conductor)

> > Charlie, ring me up the new one, would you, for Helen.

> (Music starts, fun, frolicking orchestral music, maybe Cuban big band sounds)

HELEN: Whoo!

> (she is dancing, smiling, twirling, clapping and maybe a high kick)

> (song ends)

> > That was swell, fellas! Are we going to have the whole team of mules? All the girls in the line up?

STAN: Sure, doll! A big production.

HELEN: Who's going to be the lead? Who's the fella?

CAL: That's just it, kid. I'm going to be in it. Just like old times! Whadya think?

HELEN: Cal, you've got a great head for this racket but you haven't danced in twenty years. You think you're up for it?

CAL: Up for it? Kid, let's dance!

(more music here, Cal takes her in his arms and they glide around the room, dancing)

See?! I still got it.

(Cal sits down next to Stan.)

HELEN: Cal you still got all the moves. But I have to think that it should be somebody who isn't twice my age. Maybe a younger guy, like Solly Bridgetower.

We just did a show down at the Paramount. Good looking guy and has a great act.

(Solly Bridgetower enters. He is close to Helen's age, fit and handsome. He is wearing casual clothes, like what a dancer might wear at a rehearsal)

SOLLY: Hello, Sweetie! Great to see you here. Are you going to be in the big number?

HELEN: That's why I brought you here. I need all the help I can get to carry this number.

(she indicates Cal and Stan, who now seem much older, compared to this young, fit couple)

SOLLY: What kind of thing is this anyway? You looking for a Romeo-type action?

(to the orchestra conductor)

Charlie, give me a one-two, would you?

(music starts and Solly dances smoothly around the stage, then stops in front of Helen to sing a showy love song. It is casual and easy flirting.)

HELEN: Awww, that's great stuff, Sol! I'm so glad you are here.

CAL: (to Solly) Listen, kid. I don't know you, but whatever Helen says, goes. So you are in. But Stan and I are still trying to work this thing out. We've got to get the motivations. All the angles, you see?

SOLLY: OK. Sure. You work it out. But if I'm going to be in this thing I've got to know one thing?

CAL: What's that?

SOLLY: Do I screw her?

CAL: (outraged) WHAT??!! What did you say?!

HELEN: For Chrisssake Sol!

SOLLY: Well, I've got to know. I have to prepare, you know.

If I am going to pre-form a sex act with her, on stage, every night for the run of the show, and on tour, well, I've just got to be ready. And prepared. You know what I mean?

CAL: What are you talking about? Sex act? On stage?!

SOLLY: Listen, Cal. You might be behind the times. I mean, when was the last time you done it with her?

CAL: She's been dead for a decade!

SOLLY: Theater is different now. People screw on stage all the time now. It's common. It's called Pre-formance Art.

CAL: NO! No. It might be a performance but it sure as hell isn't art!

SOLLY: Stan, Cal, listen. You are writing this thing now. I'm just saying that I'd like to screw her. Every night. You can just write it in. Part of the show.

HELEN: Solly, you listen now. You might want to do it with me but that doesn't mean that I want to do it with you. I've been screwed over in the theater so many times, I've lost count. I can see this one coming a mile away! I tell you.

(Naomi wakes at this point. She looks around.)

NAOMI: You alright, hon? You need anything?

CAL: Maybe a cup of coffee. Would you?

NAOMI: Sure.

(Naomi gets up, makes a cup of coffee, brings it to Cal then goes back and sits down.)

(She watches the happenings from here)

HELEN: Solly, I'm not just some piece of cheesecake in a glitter bikini for you to ogle and fondle.

(during this she takes off the headdress, takes off her shoes and hangs them limply on a hat stand. She takes up Cal's old-man robe from a hook and wraps herself in it, tying it at the waist. Cal, Stan and Solly watch her transition from glamourous showgirl to a real-life woman with her own vitality.)

I was in the business for thirty years, you know. Pregnant, twice, during show tours. Paid the bills. And paid my dues. So I don't have to take a bunch of guff from you, Solly.

Cal, we had such a great life. I loved you so much. Do you know that? Do you know how much I admired you too? You were the best. The crowds, oh! The crowds. They loved you so much. It was the best

	thing in the world to be dancing with you, zooming around a big stage, with the music really going, and the crowds!
STAN:	The roar of the greasepaint and the smell of the crowds.
HELEN:	That's right! You could just feel the heat from the people when a really great number came on. But you know what, I've been working on my own thing. Getting ready to put up my thing.
CAL:	What do you mean? What's that?
HELEN:	I want to do a one-woman show.
STAN:	Yeah? That sounds great. What's it about.
HELEN:	It's going to be a profile of Bella Abzug.
CAL:	What?! Bella Abzug?
HELEN:	Yeah. Like this.

(Helen becomes Bella Abzug, a prominent attorney and politician who organized for the rights of women in America during the 1970s. She is direct but charming, with humor. Maybe hunched forward some. If there is a floppy hat in the robe pocket, she puts it on now.)

(as Bella) What the hell am I doing here? Is that you Cal? I thought I recognized you.

CAL:	Hello, Bee. How are you?
HELEN:	What do you care, Cal? You've never thought for two seconds about the condition of women in this world.
CAL:	That's not fair…
HELEN:	Do you remember when we first met, Cal? Remember what you said to me?
CAL:	(hangs his head) We don't have to get into that, Bee.
HELEN:	(addressing everybody else on stage and the audience)

It was 1977. You were doing a musical production for the National Women's Conference in Chicago.

STAN:	I remember that one. Great crowd. Great crowd, those broads.
HELEN:	(disgusted) Stan. Broads? Really? Broads?
STAN:	Sorry.
HELEN:	I was getting ready to give a keynote address. I was in the middle of a national book tour, pushing my new book at the time. Then I was heading to DC to lobby the congressman from Delaware following the Women's Conference.

> (to Cal) And as I am standing offstage, rehearsing my speech, the musical number was finishing up. You came through the wings and saw me waiting to go on.
>
> You looked at my dress and said, "Nice tits!" and kept on walking.

CAL: (shakes his head) I'm sorry.

HELEN: And that has been my life's work, summed up in one line: Nice tits! Not my policy work, my organizing, our advocating for women and children. We spent our lives fighting for equality and recognition. But what did you recognize? Nice tits.

CAL: I'm sorry, Bee. I was a jerk. I still am, I think.

HELEN: (Straightening up, now Helen again)

(She takes off the robe, hangs it on the hat rack, puts on her shoes.)

> Oh, Cal. You were sweet. You were so sweet to me. But.. you weren't, you weren't... fooling around on me, were you? Were you?

CAL: Never. I didn't even know who she was at the time. Surrounded by showgirls my whole life, that's the kind of thing you say.

HELEN: I don't blame you. A girl's gotta know if she's got punch to her look. If you're on stage, on display, it's good to know you got the punch.

STAN: Say Cal, what was your favorite number, years ago, you know?

CAL: Easy. Yankee Doodle.

STAN: Really paid the bills for you?

CAL: No, that's not it. It was a good song to let people know that I believed in the country, that everybody believed in America. The real land of the free. Real liberty.

SOLLY: But that's not super modern anymore. Maybe they liked it back in the day, like old-school, but today? Don't know. Don't think it would take hold now. Like that.

CAL: Probably not.

(here a melancholy version of Yankee Doodle plays. Helen and Solly sway, side by side)

> I don't mind getting old. I don't mind that I won't be around too long. I just wish it was more fun to go to the theater. Everybody is so serious – and hairy, and naked. Everybody is so much for themselves now.

Maybe it's always been this way but the idea of liberty didn't just mean 'I get mine!'

It used to be that people looked out for each other, not just pour all the money into the pockets of the Rockefellers.

And, - and this is not the currency of the day, but I'm old enough to speak my mind - it's about the responsibility of the government to help all Americans. It just makes me heartsick.

What happened to Entertainment? Song and Dance? A love story with some comedy.

SOLLY: Look, times have changed. People have a lot of options now. You can change the channel on TV without getting up. People have computers. Cal, you have an iPad. You can watch whatever you want.

HELEN: But Solly, that's the thing. We gave so much to the theater. We sang. We danced. We wrote and produced. We entertained a whole lotta folks. That's a good thing. It's a good thing we done.

CAL: I know, dear. I know. But I want to go back. I want it like it was. Now I start to write a show and I get halfway through and I have already forgotten what it was about. I want to see some theater, but everything is closed.

All my vaudeville pals are gone now. All dead. There is just me. Just me.

HELEN: I miss you, Cal.

CAL: (choking up) I miss you too, doll.

There is nothing to do now. No place to go. Nobody comes around anymore. I'm stuck in this coffin night and day (indicating the apartment).

I want to get up and dance again. Dance with you, darling, but now, I can barely get out of this damned chair.

STAN: Hey, hey! Cheer up there. OK. Who was the funniest act you ever saw?

CAL: Easy. Will Rogers. He'd have them eating out of his hand, inside ten seconds.

STAN: Ha! I remember. He said, I'm not a member of any organized political party…

SOLLY: (he becomes Will Rogers) I'm a Democrat!

CAL: Ha!

SOLLY: (as Will Rogers, moving around in Rogers' rambling style, faux-bumpkin)

Cal, how are you, old partner? I see you talking to the beautiful Miss Helen here. I'm here to clear one thing up for you. It's been weighing on me.

It's just that there are two theories about how to argue with a woman. Neither works.

CAL: Ha!

SOLLY: It's true. But my Pappy told me when I was real small, when you find yourself in a hole, quit digging!

CAL: Ho!

SOLLY: Cal, you're sitting here moaning about how you want to be young again.

Some people try to turn back the odometers. Not me. I want people to know "why" I look this way.

I've traveled the long way round - and some of these roads weren't paved.

CAL: Heh!

SOLLY: You know there is the old question about whether animals have souls.

I don't know if we'll ever get to the bottom of that one.

But if there are no dogs in heaven, why, when I die, I want to go where they went.

CAL: Me too!

SOLLY: Cal, I see you there and I realize that there are three kinds of men in the world.

There's the ones that learn by readin'.

Then there's the a few who learn by observation.

The rest of them fellas have to pee on the electric fence for themselves.

CAL: Ha-ha!

SOLLY: Just remember that everything is funny, if it is happening to somebody else.

You know, it takes quite a while, but I guess that most men are about as happy as they make up their minds to be.

But things ain't what they used to be, and probably never was.

CAL: Heh!

SOLLY: So Cal, you are sitting here crying the blues. But remember, even if you are on the right track, if you just sit there, you'll still get run over!

Good night folks!

(Solly exits)

STAN: Ah, he was the best.

CAL: (sighs) Yep. Say, hon, you remember this number?

(sings Once I was a Star)

Once I was a star…

Hero of the stage,

And screen.

Now life is as we are…

Waiting here to turn the page,

And leave.

What was it all for?

Is it the same in every Age,

And day?

I wish that you were here,

Because you alone can gauge

My heart,

My dear.

Oh I wish upon a star,

Twinkling at the evening's edge,

To be so young again,

Kissing you,

You, again.

HELEN: That was lovely, Cal. We'll be kissing again, real soon. I miss you, love.

CAL: I miss you too, love.

HELEN: (Blows a kiss and exits)

STAN: (shakes his head) You know what your problem is?

CAL: What? What's my problem?

STAN: That you got no problems. You're rich. You have this good woman who looks after you. Nobody is expecting you to be someplace, on time. Nobody is waiting for your latest number. The only one waiting, is you.

CAL: For the end.

STAN: Well – maybe quit stalling. Get on with it. Close the show.

CAL: Curtains?

STAN: No encores for this show.

CAL: Maybe you are right. Maybe it's time to strike the set and send the orchestra home.

STAN: You are not writing a big new show. Nobody is offering you a script. There is no more show for you.

CAL: I don't think I can do it. An 'exit stage left' sounds easy enough, but how do you do it?

STAN: You just get up, and go.

(Stan gets up, nods at Cal, then exits)

CAL: (softly singing Once I was a Star, closes his eyes and nods off. *Dead?*)

NAOMI: You alright, Mr. Cal?

(she wakes him)

CAL: Oh, hmmph… Yes. Yeah. Crazy dream.

NAOMI: You have to get ready. Miss Grace is coming back and she's got a surprise for you.

CAL: A surprise? What is it?

NAOMI: Oh, I won't tell. I won't ruin her surprise.

(Knock at the door. Grace comes in with Solly Bridgetower)

GRACE: Grandpa Cal, I want you to meet my fiancé. This is William Sullivan. We are going to be married in the spring. I wanted to tell you as soon as we decided.

CAL: What a wonderful surprise! I can't wait. It will be a real treat to put on a tie and dance with you in your wedding dress. It's really something great to look forward to. Congratulations. William, is it?

SOLLY: (as William Sullivan) Yes sir. But everybody calls me Bill.

CAL: A pleasure to know you, Bill. You take care of my favorite lady here.

NAOMI: Now Mr. Cal, I thought I was your favorite lady. That's what you always tell me anyhow.

CAL: (laughing) Now you have caught me out. I am pleased for you both. I just wish your Grandma Helen was here to see you two. I know she's smiling down on us right now.

GRACE: We can't stay though. William's mother is expecting us for lunch. You take care of yourself and I will be around to visit again real soon.

CAL: Alright dear.

(William and Grace exit through the door)

NAOMI: I have that coffee for you, Mr. Cal.

CAL: Wonderful, Naomi. Thank you.

(both sit side by side, sipping coffee)

(end)

Sword In The Heart

By Rick Regan

Setting is fictional, British-style kingdom of roughly the Arthurian time, ca. 1000 – 1500 AD .

<u>Characters:</u>

KING,   getting older but has no heir

First MINISTER, aide to the King

WIZARD,   aide to the King

CAROL,   wife of First MINISTER, mother of Edward

EDWARD,   soldier, son of Carol

GABRIELLE,   mother of David

DAVID,   blacksmith, son of Gabrielle

<u>Players:</u>

King   Ed Backes

Minister   BT McNicholl

Wizard   Maura Vincent

Edward   Rick Regan

Carol   JC Marshall

Gabrielle   Lyn Peticolas

David   JC Marshall

Scene 1: King's Throne Room, King by himself

KING:	Today is a glorious, wonderous day. Today will be the great and joyous day when my son is born by my queen. He will be the prince and, one day, the king.

All I can do is wait. Wait. Wait. Wait. Wait.

While the sun spins around and the stars pivot, I sit and wait. Why is it suffering to wait? I, as King, am to direct action, not just wait for Fate to have her cruel way with me.

MINISTER	(enters) My King! My lord!

KING	Minister! Oh joy! Tell me the joyous news!

MINISTER:	Sire... The queen has died.

KING:	Oh! And the baby, my son?

MINISTER:	The baby is dead.

KING:	My day of joy is crushed! My heart is pierced by the sword of cruel Fate!

MINISTER:	I am so sorry, sir.

KING:	Minister, please fetch the Wizard. Perhaps she can help.

MINISTER:	(exits)

KING:	(alone) What can I do? What can be done?

WIZARD:	(enters with Minister)

Sir, the Minister has told me the sad news of the Queen and the child. I am so sorry.

KING:	What can I do? What can be done?

WIZARD:	I have already spoken to the physicians. The baby seems to have died some days ago. I am very sorry. The Queen herself had lost so much blood in her struggle that she could not be revived or saved. She died in her courageous battle.

KING:	I am heart broken and tired. Thank you for your efforts and sympathy.

I will retire to my room now, with the crushing weight of my sadness for my Queen. Alone.

Please re-join me here in the morning. We must discuss what is to be done about my succession plan tomorrow.

(all exit)

Scene 2: King's chambers

KING: (alone) Wait. Wait. Wait. Now I wait for my waiters. The night has come and gone, and I slept not a wink. Alone now, without the queen, my dear queen.

MINISTER: (enters) Good morning, sir. I am glad to see you are revived.

KING: Minister. I wish that I could revive us all.

WIZARD: (enters) My lord, how are you this morning?

KING: Wizard, do you not know? Do you not see into your crystal ball, to see into my heart? Or is it too dark, too black, without moon or stars? Without wife or son?

MINISTER: Sir, I have been thinking about the problem of there being no heir. I am afraid as word circulates, our enemies will see an opportunity to attack us.

KING: Bluetooth and his pirates may try to attack, but our garrisons are brimming with well-trained men, eager to wet their blades in the bloody brains of his illiterate dogs. And they know well my wrath, my power. They should fear me, attacking, sweeping them back into the chilly sea.

MINISTER: Of course, my king, but I will send out some men to watch for anything unusual.

KING: We will do more than that. I think it may be a good season for killing. I think we have been at peace too long. I think we do not wait for war to come to us. We shall be the engine of war. Of conquest.

WIZARD: My king, the season is late, and quite wet for marching armies. Perhaps caution should be the guide.

MINISTER: My king, I think that any war led by you would be swift and just. We can drive the devils away before the first frost.

KING: Minister, ready me a plan of attack, with the locations of the enemy.

MINISTER: (moves to leave) Yes, sir. Right away.

KING: Wait, Minister. For there is one other business for which I need your eyes and ears.

MINISTER: Anything, sir.

KING: I need a plan for an heir. Should I find a new queen? I am afraid I do not have time. I am not an old man but if I am to war, I do not have time to wed.

MINISTER: Or to bed.

WIZARD: Sir, if I may, I have given this some thought and I have an idea for you.

KING: Please proceed.

WIZARD: My lord, for succession of a king, the people must believe in the divine provenance of the prince. It must be shown that the new king is in direct line from God, through the king to himself. He must be absolutely in the perfect grace of God. Like yourself, sir.

KING: And a son would do this.

WIZARD: So too would a man of your choosing.

KING: My choosing?

WIZARD: If we were to produce a miracle that shows this man to be worthy of the heavenly blessing, then the people would accept him as your successor to be king.

MINISTER: And how to we produce a miracle, Wizard?

WIZARD: We make a contest where all men can challenge themselves but only the divinely appointed one will succeed.

KING: I am not sure any of us here would pass that test.

WIZARD: My lord, if you looked out at your vast lands and many people, if you thought of all the sons of all the families in the land, who would you choose to be king?

KING: Me.

MINISTER: I think he means, who to follow you as king, sir.

KING: Ah, yes. Let me think on it.

WIZARD: And I have in mind a particular miracle.

KING: What is it?

WIZARD: I would prefer to speak it to you alone sir. There is a secret to how it is won.

MINISTER: I will leave you. (moves to exit)

WIZARD: It could be the center of a feasting celebration of the late Queen, sir. A grieving and mourning of all the people. And there would be the miracle.

KING: Minister. Wait. I want you to hear.

WIZARD: Sir, are you sure?

KING: Wizard, my Minister, like you, I hold in my utmost confidence. Please, explain the miracle.

WIZARD: As you wish. The miracle is the Sword in the Stone. The man who can pull the sword from the stone becomes divinely approved to be the prince.

MINISTER: And how do you put a sword in a stone?

WIZARD: That is my business. But it is not just any sword. My lord, I will need your sword.

KING: My sword?!

WIZARD: Yes, of course. It is to be the coronation of the new prince. It cannot be just the sword of some sergeant of the fort. It must be the divine sword of the king. My lord, will you give me your sword?

KING: I will not! Not over my beating heart will I surrender my sword!

WIZARD: But sir, consider what it is that we are trying to achieve. Think of the one whom you anoint, whom you choose. He alone will have the secret to remove the sword. All else will fail.

MINISTER: My lord, I do see the wisdom of the Wizard. If you just picked a man, then the people will say, No, I do not like him. Pick someone else.

WIZARD: But if it is that we use the miracle, the people will know that it is their destiny to have this king, and you will have chosen the man yourself.

KING: Wizard, how is this to be done? What is the secret.

WIZARD: My lord, it is just so. I heat a large stone until a crack forms, big enough for the blade to go in. When the stone cools, it seizes around the blade, making it impossible to remove. But if, instead of pulling, a man hammers the handle, the stone itself will split, and the sword is released. But, my lord, no one should know of the secret. Only the man who you choose should be told the key to the kingdom.

KING: Minister, I want you to send someone you trust to ride out to the forts and garrisons, all the camps of our fighting men, and tell them that we will have a great contest for the divine anointment of the prince. Tell them it is my will, as I am grieving the late Queen.

And, Minister hear me, tell no one the secret. I will think on my choice and I alone, hear me, I alone shall choose who shall be the prince. I alone shall tell them the secret of the sword in the stone. Minister, hear me, do I have your oath that you will tell no one?

MINISTER: On my honor, my lord.

KING: More than that, Minister. On your life! Do you understand me?

MINISTER: In the utmost, my lord.

KING: Then, Minister, make it so!

MINISTER: Yes, your regency! (exits)

KING: Hmmm...

WIZARD: Was that wise, sir? He will play his own game with this knowledge.

KING: I play my own games too, Wizard.

WIZARD: Aye, sir. (exits)

KING: Hmmm...

WIZARD: Was that wise, sir? He will play his own game with this knowledge.

KING: I play my own games too, Wizard.

WIZARD: Aye, sir. (exits)

Scene 3: Minister's home

MINISTER:	(enters) Wife! Wife!
CAROL:	(enters) My brave and loyal husband, what news have you of the king?
MINISTER:	Wife, I have found the key, the way, the entrée for young Edward to be, to be... Wife, king!
CAROL:	So! So. It is time. The time has come. Finally!
MINISTER:	I will be the kingmaker. And you will be the mother of the king. King Edward.
CAROL:	All of it has paid off, my love. And you will make it happen. How is it to be, dearest?
MINISTER:	I have been given an order by the king to gather all the great men of the land to test themselves at a feat of strength, pulling the King's sword from a stone. Yet only I know the secret of the test. We must tell no one that Edward will be the chosen one. I will tell him, the day before the contest and not a moment before, or hint of the fact.
CAROL:	You are the wisest man in all the world.
MINISTER:	Do you swear to me that you will hold this secret to your heart, even to our son? You must not breathe a word of it.
CAROL:	For you my dearest love, I pledge all and everything. Everything!
MINISTER:	Bring Edward to me.
CAROL:	(exits, returns with EDWARD, their son)
MINISTER:	Edward, I have a task for you, or rather the king has requested your aid, your help and great strength for a great duty.
EDWARD:	Father, I am back to my regiment tomorrow. I cannot take up some task for you, or the king.
MINISTER:	Do not say that, my son. We, this family, me, you and your mother are loyal to our king above God himself. Do you understand me? Great opportunity awaits you on this quest.
EDWARD:	What can be so great as this? What is the command of heaven, from that old goat, the king?
CAROL:	(slaps Edward) You will never speak ill of the king, or I will strike you dead! Or you will see me on the other side of the veil of shadows, in the grave weeping for your soul.
EDWARD:	Mother, what loyalty do you have for that old crab? The men in my garrison say that he has never led a battle, never won a war and is a fool besides.

MINISTER: Son, I am the minister. You do not know of the terrible horror of war. Our king has made and kept a peace that I hope to you know for a generation. Glory in war is only a fool's gold of young men who have not smelled the death and heard the dying.

EDWARD: Father, if you say it is true then it must be true. But you see that it is a new age, a new time. The day of the old is passing and the time of the young is now. Do you see that father, or are you so far inside the king's bedchamber that you do not feel the tide moving?

CAROL: Do not speak to the Minister in that way!

MINISTER: Son, listen to me! Cool your overheated head. I have a special quest for you.

EDWARD: Father, I must go in the morning.

MINISTER: You will go where I tell you to go! I am the First Minister of the King!

I am directed to send a trusted soldier to all the garrisons, forts and camps, to bring a message of a great feast. This will be the feast of the grieving for the recent queen.

EDWARD: Father, you must be joking!

MINISTER: Listen to me, son. At the feast there will be a test, of all the men, to decide whom God wishes to be the new prince and successor to the king.

EDWARD: A test?

MINISTER: Yes, the king and the Wizard are trusting in God, that whomever the Almighty selects to be the new king will be one to seize the sword from the stone. And you, my son, are the chosen one, to deliver the message far and wide, to all the men of the land who wish to be king.

EDWARD: I wish to be king, father.

MINISTER: And I wish to be king, son.

CAROL: Who will be king?

MINISTER: Only I will decide. God will agree in his eternal time.

But son, you must go tomorrow, with the charter from the king to bring all the greatest men of the land to the feast. Will you go?

EDWARD: Upon your command, Minister.

Scene 4: King's chambers

KING: (alone)

Do I make war, or peace? Is my legacy my actions or my country as I leave it? Prosperous, healthy and peaceful, or struggling under the lash of war, or conquest if we should fail?

My father was king, and his father was king. And I... I... am I king? Am I divinely anointed to the mandate of heaven? The crown is warm but heavy.

MINISTER: (entering)

My lord, there is a woman here who seeks an audience. I have tried to send her away, but she will not be swept aside. She is the wife of a blacksmith in a near village. She says if I mention her name, you will see her.

KING: What is this name?

MINISTER: Gabrielle, wife of blacksmith. Daughter of a blacksmith.

KING: Ah. Yes. Ah. Yes. Minister this is a delicate matter.

MINISTER: Of course, sir. I will be very attentive.

KING: No, I must speak to her myself. Alone. Fetch her and then leave us.

MINISTER: Yes, king. (exits)

GABRIELLE: (enters) My lord, how good it is to see you again.

KING: Gabrielle. It is you.

GABRIELLE: Certainly, it is me. I come to say that I have heard the sad news of the Queen's passing. I send you my deepest sympathies.

KING: That is truly kind. But why have you made this visit today?

GABRIELLE: I know you are busy. I know that there are many in the court who tempt you and eat up your time. How frantic you must be, all the time tempted and tugged.

I come on a simple errand, a simple favor to ask of my friend, Gerald.

KING: Remember I am king.

GABRIELLE: I say your name because I remember you. I remember your name. I remember your face, remember your body. I remember our bodies. Do you remember?

KING: Oh, I see. This is a request, at the point of a knife.

GABRIELLE: No, Gerald, you misread me. I am here on a simple purpose. A simple request for you. I want my son to be admitted to your contest to be king.

KING: It is not a contest. It is a miracle. It is the decision of God, not me. It will be His hand that pulls the sword from the stone. Only God decides.

GABRIELLE: Perhaps that is so, my king. Perhaps that is so...

But this is for my son. This is for our son, David. I want him to be in the parade to pull the sword.

KING: Our son? You married a blacksmith. Surely, he is the son of the blacksmith.

GABRIELLE: Gerald, I have been loyal to you for twenty-two years. I have not uttered a word of our... past love.

I have been loyal to you. I am asking for you to be loyal to me. Not even me. Loyal to David, to your son.

KING: Gabbie, he is a blacksmith. Do you think I do not know of him? I have followed every step the lad has taken.

If I could, I would have... I would have done everything.

GABRIELLE: But instead you did nothing.

Do you not remember me, our time, our love? Have you forgotten me?

KING: Sweetest, dearest girl. Have I forgotten? How could I ever forget? I think of you in the morning when I see the stars before dawn. I see a ripple in a stream, and I think of you. I think of your body. I think of your hair. I think of your eyes and I think of your smile. I am lifted away from the world, in a dream of contented happiness when I think of your smile.

I never knew what it was to want a lover, to want a woman to have my children until I met you. Until I knew you. So warm and firm and glorious, I have wanted you every day from the first day I met you. And to want you is to want to know you, as you, the loving heart and the mind that understands all the world that I do not understand.

I desire your body. And I am over-awed by your mind. I am overcome by all of you.

GABRIELLE: But you did nothing. I married a blacksmith in the village because you would do nothing for me. I am a poor woman in one of your small villages. And you, Gerald, are king.

KING: Dear one...

GABRIELLE: I come to ask for our son to be in the list of those who will attempt the test. That is all.

KING: But Gab, he is a blacksmith, and an apprentice at that. He is not fit to be king.

GABRIELLE: And were you? Are you even now? How have you lived with your sin?

Your sin with me. Your carnality. Your gluttony. Your greed, for my body, for my smile. How greedy you were. Even now.

How many more sins? The lies. The betrayal, of me, of our son.

The vanity of your glorious rise. The theft of so much from so many. Taxes? For the king? Theft! Do you have murder on your soul as well?

KING: Oh, Gabrielle. Do not be like this.

GABRIELLE: Like this? Like what? You want me preening and naked for you, for your lust and your greed?

You would have another man's wife as well, wouldn't you?

Well, what sin is it today that I must bear, that I must suffer at your hands, grubby, grasping, greed hands?

KING: Oh, Gabrielle. To touch your beautiful body again. I am unquenched in my desire for you.

GABRIELLE: No! I should have said that long ago.

No. No to you. No to your toadies, like that Minister.

His eyes did delight upon my bosom, they did. Is he greedy and grasping like you? Of course, he is. He is loyal to you.

No. No. No, I come here to secure a place in line for our son. Our son David! Do it, Gerald. Do it.

If you owe me anything, it is this. Our sin, that I bear as well, our son, that I bore as well, we carry together. Tell your flunky man to put David on the list. Do it.

KING: Minister! Minister!

MINISTER: (entering) My lord.

KING: This fine lady has made a very persuasive argument that her son, the blacksmith David, should be on the list of those to attempt the sword test. I believe that if God wills it then I would be mistaken to refuse. Make it so, Minister.

MINISTER: But sir, we have a list of the finest men of the young generation. Is this man, her son, to be prepared in advance?

KING: No. He is to be in line to try, prepared as any man. Now leave us.

MINISTER: As you wish. (exits)

GABRIELLE: Thank you, Gerald.

KING: It is you I am to thank. You have raised our son well. I am proud of him, without reason of course because you have done it all. Nonetheless I am proud and pleased. It is my vanity. Will you come again, dearest?

GABRIELLE: We shall see how the contest goes, won't we?

Is there anything I should know or tell David?

KING: Pull hard! That is all. Pull hard!

GABRIELLE: Goodbye Gerald. (exits)

KING: (alone)   Goodbye my dearest love. My fondest memory.

Scene 5: Minister's home

CAROL: (alone at a table, peeling an apple)

The shame of it. The corruption. The poor, lovely Queen.

But if we are in the river, why not let the river take us, instead of carting our goods with donkeys and a wagon?

MINISTER: (enters) Good wife, our son is away, these many days now, on his quest for the king.

CAROL: Good husband tell me. What is the miracle of the sword?

MINISTER: I have sworn my oath to the king that I will not breathe a word, and I will not.

CAROL: Good husband, you have said that Edward will be king. How is that so?

MINISTER: Wife, you are an uneducated mule. You will know what you know because I say it, not because you know it.

If I say that I will not reveal the secret to any soul that means you too. That is enough.

But I have told our son Edward the secret. Soon he will be king.

CAROL: A mule? A mule? That you mount and ride around our bed whenever it suits you?

MINISTER: Good wife, you are a beast of service. You are here to serve your husband. Me. Trust that I will do you no harm. But I do insist that you behave and obey.

CAROL: I do trust you. I have trusted you. But, good husband, surely, I am more to you than a mule. We have mules in the barn. Would you put me out there with the animals?

MINISTER: I would put you, good wife, where you are best used, for service. If it is my pleasure to ride you, for my own satisfaction, then I will keep you in the bed. If you are tired or bitter or disagreeable, then perhaps your place will soon be with the other beasts. Mind your ways, wife.

CAROL: Husband, I am as agreeable as any woman. You and I have built a life and a family together. Yet you think me just a beast... of service.

MINISTER: Service is a noble task, wife. Submit and serve. And God is pleased.

CAROL: Henry. I am your wife. I am not a beast for your pleasure or service.

MINISTER: Now hear me, wife! You will do as I say. You will obey and serve! You will obey and serve, or I will bring the lash upon your back. I will count the strokes as I count your disobedient sins.

CAROL: If you strike one hair on my head, I will wager my soul with murder. I will put the matter to the Almighty. And let him tally your sins, on your bloody death!

MINISTER: You shall not go near so much as a dull butter knife! I will turn you over my knee right now!

CAROL: Minister! There is something you should know.

MINISTER: Speak! Mule.

CAROL: Edward is not your progeny. Edward is the blood line of our king.

MINISTER: You deceitful harlot! You are a lying wench!

CAROL: Your cruel and dirty mind have you licking the king's fingers. But I have had him in my bed! Our bed.

MINISTER: You back-stabbing whore! I will hear none of it.

CAROL: He has had me here. Many times! Pounding me like a mad man, like grain crushed at the mill. He leaves me defeated and weeping with his cruel handling of me.

MINISTER: You are the pouring the Devil's words in my ear! You are a screeching harpy.

CAROL: Even when the Queen was dying, bleeding, dying to bring him an heir, I took his body, his lust, his passion. And do you know why?

Because you are loyal to the king and I am loyal to you.

Now you call me a mule one more time!

MINISTER: Slutty whore of a wife. Deceitful snake! Your immodesty would shame a she-wolf. I am shamed by the hideous sight of you. Even a camel has pride but you what pride have you?

CAROL: I have the pride of our son. The son of the king. Not you.

Edward is my pride. And I want you to make him king.

MINISTER: I will no more make him king that I will let you live to see the sunrise. You are dead to me!

(Minister chases Carol out the door)

CAROL: Ayyyy! Murder! Ayyyyy!

(runs out the door, chased by Minister)

Scene 6: King's Chambers

KING: Today is the day. The men at arms have been gathered. They have all been pulling at the Wizard's sword, and as he said, none have mastered the stone. Would I have passed the test? Would God favor me, again, if I pulled at the sword, my own sword?

WIZARD: (enters) My king, how do you fare this morning?

KING: Wizard, I count myself mightily abused by so many men that think they can be king. I look and see the ranks of them, soldiers, farmers, even bankers, who think themselves up to the task. But you have provided an excellent test, Wizard. None have mastered it.

WIZARD: That is precisely the point, sir. All must test themselves - and fail. All must measure themselves against the will of God, and find God's will for them... wanting.

Then when the champion of your choosing does the trick, all will know that they were bested by the choice of heaven. Each man will not have been defeated, but rather each man must acknowledge the pure grace of God, and their loyalty to the new king.

KING: Perhaps that is so.

WIZARD: But that is not why I have come, sir. I come to ask you something. I have heard rumors of enemy armies gathering, the storms of war.

KING: What have you come to ask?

WIZARD: My lord, I wonder if there is anything that I should know, that God should know.

KING: What should you know?

WIZARD: Are there any sins, my lord? Any sins that have not been reconciled, atoned?

KING: What is this matter, Wizard? Are you the priest now as well?

WIZARD: My king, I am your loyal servant. I look and I learn, and I endeavor to serve you well.

KING: And this sword business is fine and well done.

WIZARD: My lord, the wisdom of God is infinite, must be infinite.

So too must be His love and mercy, infinite.

But also, my lord, infinite is the justice of heaven.

KING: Justice? What is this, Wizard? Do not speak in riddles.

WIZARD: My lord, the justice of the Almighty must balance the weight of our sins against the punishment for our disobedience to God, perfect and infinite. Do you understand, my lord?

KING: No. I do not understand. What is the punishment you speak of?

WIZARD: My lord, see this, that the wise prophets and priests describe the punishment of the wicked. And, sir, I wonder if you have been wicked.

For if you have forsaken the oath of the crown, to serve God and country faithfully, then our miracle may go awry.

The hand of divine justice may pierce our heart with the sword of punishment. Do you see, my lord?

KING: I see this.

I have lost my queen. I have lost my son. I have enemies gathering at frontiers. And a line of men all think themselves worthy to be king, to draw the sword and think themselves already a better king than me.

I hear you prattling on about sin and justice, trying to save my soul but, hear me now, my soul was lost long ago, crushed under the weight of the crown.

My sins? My petty sins? God should be held to account for my suffering. If He has infinite justice, He would end my suffering, my torment, and help our kingdom to be proud and prosperous, for His great glory. That is the legacy I seek, to build a peaceful, just and prosperous kingdom, under God's blessing.

My sins are of no matter. If I have betrayed God, it was done purely for the kingdom.

WIZARD: Yes, of course, my lord. Your wisdom too is indeed infinite.

So, who have you chosen to know the secret of the stone? Who shall be prince to you?

KING: Ah, Wizard this is the test of all my ability, wisdom and experience.

Who is the rightly suited man to lead the country into the new age, and the battles to come?

WIZARD: Yes, my lord. Who?

KING: I have chosen a young man who is dear to my heart, who I have known from his earliest days. You know him as well.

I am choosing Edward, son of the Minister. He is loyal, experienced and smart. He is well respected by his men, and has his father, the Minister, to guide him.

I choose Edward. I have spoken with him this morning and I have told him, and him alone, the secret of the stone.

WIZARD: Certainly, a wise choice, my king.

MINISTER: (entering) My lord. Wizard. How is the feasting and grieving?

KING: Everything proceeds apace, Minister. How are things with you, this fine day?

MINISTER: My wife has taken ill, my lord. I am gravely concerned about her condition.

WIZARD: Is it a breathing disorder? Perhaps I have a compound to relieve her.

MINISTER: No, Wizard. She had a fall, in the yard last night. She was gathering apples in the evening and fell from a great perch. I am stunned and worried for her.

KING: I will make a visit to her myself.

MINISTER: There is no need for that, my king. I think some rest and time away from folk is best for her now.

KING: As you wish, but I would sorely miss her if she is not at the feast today.

MINISTER: She will be right as rain, right along, sir.

KING: Send her my blessings.

MINISTER: That and more.

KING: Minister, I have news for you as well. I have chosen a champion for the contest today. The person who will be prince, and then king.

MINISTER: Who will that be, my lord?

KING: Your son, Edward. I thought you would be pleased.

MINISTER: (enraged, rushes the king with a sword)

My son?! You lying son of a bitch!

You were wearing out my wife like a street trollop! All this time!

And I was loyal to you.

And now, you want to promote Edward, your bastard son to be king?

I will see you dead first!

KING: (without sword, defenseless) Ah! Back! Scoundrel!

MINISTER: (on top of king, attempts to stab King, wounds King)

Argh!

WIZARD: (swings staff and disarms Minister) Away, fiend!

KING: (grabs Minister's sword, stands above Minister, then skewers MINISTER)

Agghhh!

MINISTER: (stabbed by the King, dies on the floor, whispers)

Bastard!

KING: (breathing heavily)

Oh God! He's dead. I did not mean to kill him. He is dead!

WIZARD: The minister tried to assassinate you, my lord.

No doubt he wanted you out of the way, to make way for himself to take the throne.

He would have snatched the sword and pulled it out of the stone himself.

He was attempting to murder the king and pull the sword for himself to be king.

KING: He was my minister for so long... I am bleeding. I bleed.

WIZARD: Let us away from here now. Let us go now into the sunlight. And mend your wound. We must oversee the test of the champions.

(both exit)

Scene 7: the Longhouse, feasting hall, filled with soldiers and men from every corner of the land

KING: (shouting, addressing the men, from the floor, bleeding from his side, bandaged by WIZARD)

Men! Today is the day of destiny. Today we put forth the Test of Champions, to let God decide who is to be my prince, and one day, your king. Let us go outside to the holy stone!

(all exit to outdoor parade ground where the stone with the King's sword is front and center)

KING: Each man shall take the challenge to pull the sword from the stone. The man who relieves the sword from the stone is the Choice of Heaven. God alone decides who shall rule our fair realm. And God alone is the judge of each man.

Men, look into your hearts. If you are unworthy, God can see. If you have the stain of sin of your soul, do not tempt God for your fate. Repent and go home!

If your heart is heavy with your past deeds and your sinful life, do not tempt God's justice, his infinite mercy and justice, for your salvation.

I am the king of our land, ruler of all here, chosen by God. In His divine wisdom He has chosen me to rule the people, the land and livestock here for all my mortal days. But my life is not eternal. Nor is yours.

If you look into your heart and know that you will get to heaven, then you are welcome here.

But a black heart, hoping for forgiveness from eternal damnation, you should not put your hand upon the sword of the sovereign. For the Lord will see that your sins are punished.

Who among you is worthy? Who steps forward?

(everyone but a small handful back away after this. The men line up and try to pull the sword out, with no success.)

(The two remainders are EDWARD, the soldier, son of CAROL, and DAVID, the blacksmith, son of GABRIELLE)

(beside the stone with the KING's sword)

EDWARD: (to DAVID) After you, good sir.

DAVID: Surely you should go first. You are the son of the First Minister.

EDWARD: I am but a humble servant of the king. I put myself last only because I am humble and loyal.

DAVID: But sir, there is nothing to it. I am a blacksmith. This is an easy matter.

EDWARD: (worried) Have you been told the secret?

DAVID: There is no secret. Just pull it out.

EDWARD: Ah, yes. No secret. Just pull it out. Please sir, I shall go after you.

DAVID: But it is nothing.

KING: (impatient, also wounded and bleeding)

(seeing his two illegitimate sons, the half-brothers, the last men standing for the test)

What is this? What is this bickering? (to Edward) Are you man enough or no?

DAVID: Sir, I will retrieve this sword for you.

(DAVID steps forward, pulls out his blacksmith hammer, whacks the end of the sword and the stone splits. He pulls the sword and raises it up to the cheering crowd)

CROWD: HURRAY! A Champion!

EDWARD: NO! That sword is to be mine! I am to be king! I am the chosen one!

(EDWARD rushes DAVID)

DAVID:

(Turns royal sword on EDWARD, who rushes into the point)

(DAVID looks at EDWARD on the sword for a moment and then drives the blade completely through EDWARD)

Take that, Minister's son! My sword now!

EDWARD: (Dying) Agh! No! I am to be king. I... am... to... be... (collapses, dies)

DAVID: (Stunned, he draw the bloody sword out of EDWARD)

KING: No! No! Edward! No.

(KING is bleeding and he hunches over EDWARD. He falls and collapses over EDWARD)

DAVID: (He looks out at crowd, raises bloody sword over his head)

CROWD: God save the King! Long live the King! God save the King!

DAVID: I am king! I am the King! I AM KING!

GABRIELLE: (in the crowd, quietly)

You are king. Now you are king. You are the king.

(end)

Good Penny

by Rick Regan, Aug. 19, 2020 Raleigh, NC

The story is about an African American woman, early 40's, who inherits her husband's small brewery in Raleigh, NC.

<u>Characters</u>:

Penny:	early 40's African American woman
Erik:	Late 40's white businessman
Brad:	Late 30's brewer
Lynn:	Penny's work associate
Cornell:	Penny's son
Aida:	Cornell's girlfriend

<u>Players</u>:

Penny:	Maura Vincent
Erik:	Rick Regan
Brad:	BT McNichol
Lynn:	JC Glanville
Cornell:	Ed Backes
Aida:	Lynn Peticolas

Scene 1

Penny and Lynn are sitting at a low table in the taproom of a small brewery

LYNN: Jesus, who do you have to kiss to get a beer around here?

PENNY: I can see why they need us. The service could certainly use some work.

BRAD: (enters, comes to table) Hey, you guys look like you could use some beer. Can I get you something?

LYNN: Is there a waitress?

BRAD: No. It's a taproom. If we had a waitress we'd be a bar. But we're not a bar. It's a brewery.

PENNY: Um, OK. How do I get a beer?

BRAD: Go to the bar and pick out whatever you want. It's on me.

LYNN: Who are you?

BRAD: I'm Brad. I'm the head brewer. I can give you as much beer as you want. I'll make more. Ha!

PENNY: I'll get something for us. (goes to bar)

LYNN: So how's business, Brad?

BRAD: I thought that's what you are going to tell me, how's business. Isn't that right?

LYNN: I guess I would just like to hear it from you first. You know, on the ground experience.

PENNY: (returns with two beers) Here we go.

BRAD: (to Penny) Your friend here was about to tell me how our business is doing. Weren't you? What's your name?

LYNN: I'm Lynn.

BRAD: (shakes her hand) I'm Brad. I'm the brewer. Ha!

LYNN: Nice to meet you.

BRAD: You're cute. You married?

LYNN: I'm available, if that's what you mean. I haven't exactly found Mister Right.

BRAD: You know any other brewers? They're swells guys! Ha! Ask Erik, he'll tell ya. We're swell guys! Listen if you guys need anything, you just go to the bar and they will take care of you. Whatever you want.

PENNY:	OK.
LYNN:	Thanks Brad.
BRAD:	No. Thank you! Ha! (goes back to the bar)
PENNY:	Well now we know who the brewer is. It's pretty good beer. I don't drink much beer because it is usually so bitter but this is really smooth.
LYNN:	He was kind of cute, don't you think?
PENNY:	Lynn, are you going to fall for a customer?
LYNN:	He's not the customer. He's just the brewer. Erik is the money guy. Plus, did you see his hands. They looked like sensitive hands.
PENNY:	Lynn, I've seen some fast movers but I don't think I've every seen a woman pick up a guy in 10-seconds. You're amazing. Ha!
LYNN:	Penny, we all need loving. You know.
PENNY:	Well I'm between things right now and I'm just trying to keep swimming so I don't drown. New job. New city. New people. It's all a lot.
ERIK:	(enters, goes to the table. Erik is in his early forties. He seems elegant and charming, wearing a blazer and creased slacks.) Hello ladies. It looks like you've gotten settled. Can I join you?
PENNY:	Of course, Mr. Prince. Please pull up a chair. It's your place after all.
ERIK:	Please call me Erik. Mr. Prince was my father to me so I always look over my shoulder to see if he snuck up behind me.
LYNN:	So I want to thank you for all the information today. The tour of production, the IT systems, the accounting information. All the reports. We have a lot of data to go through already.
PENNY:	Erik, if I may, what is your back of the envelope sense of the situation, as it is now? And going forward?
ERIK:	Well pretty clearly the place has no profits. But excellent beer. I think that with some clever marketing can drive this place to profitability.
LYNN:	I'd say that's pretty spot on.
PENNY:	Agreed. So what are we here for if you know all this already.
ERIK:	I need your firm to do a study for me to determine how do we get there.

LYNN: Well that's what we're good at.

ERIK: I'm a money guy, not a beer guy.

PENNY: Erik, if I may, I see two issues right away.

ERIK: Go ahead.

PENNY: First, we are the only two women in here. That's half of the market who you are not reaching.

ERIK: And the second?

PENNY: The second is that there are no people of color here.

LYNN: Except you.

PENNY: Wait! What?! (Penny looks down at her hands)

               Wait, I'm black? All this time… No wonder, the reactions I get…

LYNN: Heh! Ok, sorry…

PENNY: No, you are right. I'm a black girl from Atlanta. With an MBA from the Ivy League.

ERIK: And that's why I wanted you on this job. I need somebody who can get to the point. Most beer is all the same but the marketing is different.

PENNY: Where does this one fit in? The dark beer?

ERIK: Oh, that's me. I told Brad I like things a little darker, with more flavor. He calls it the Brown Bomber.

PENNY: (flustered, not sure if Erik is hitting on her) Well, we'll try to do our best.

ERIK: Did you meet Brad, by the way?

LYNN: Yes, he's nice.

ERIK: He's an excellent brewer but not much of a business man. He just likes to make beer.

PENNY: What do you mean, not much of a businessman?

ERIK: He's the owner.

LYNN: I thought you were the owner.

ERIK: No. I hired your firm to make the study. I'm just a consultant.

PENNY: So you are not the owner?

ERIK: No, I'm a friend of Brad's. I'll probably be the one putting the money in to keep it going. But I'd like a roadmap of how to keep from losing my investment.

PENNY: Erik, we haven't done the study yet but I can already see what's going to happen. I've been a business

	financial consultant for the last decade and I have seen this play out many times before.
ERIK:	Well, now I really am getting my money's worth. What does it look like to you.
PENNY:	First, let me ask you about how you feel about being in the beer business?
ERIK:	But I'm not in the beer business. I am a finance guy.
PENNY:	Once you put the money in, you are in the beer business. And if there is no follow through, the money will just get spent. And a year from now, or eighteen months maybe, you'll be having a conversation with Brad about the money and he won't have it.
LYNN:	Penny!
ERIK:	I'm all ears. Go on.
PENNY:	If our study is not going to be used, then I would advise not investing in the business.
LYNN:	Jesus, Penny!
ERIK:	It's OK. I'm not afraid of straight talk. Especially from somebody who knows their business.
PENNY:	Thank you. But let me ask you again, how do you feel about being in the beer business?
ERIK:	Well... I don't know...
PENNY:	Because it would be cheaper for you to just buy the brewery now. What do you think?
ERIK:	Let me think about this. Are you still willing to do the market study?
LYNN:	We definitely want to do the study for you.
PENNY:	But if you think there will be an ownership change, perhaps it would take a different form. Don't you agree?
ERIK:	I do agree. I also think I need you on this case. You now know more about my business than I do.
PENNY:	That's why we're here.
ERIK:	OK, listen. You guys get to work on the study. I need to know everything that I need to know. And I'm going to need your help with all of it. I'm impressed.
PENNY:	Thank you.
LYNN:	Thank you. We can have a timeline generated by the end of the week.
ERIK:	Good. Let's get together again at the end of the week. And I'll talk to Brad.

BRAD: (appearing at the table) How's it going, you guys? Maximizing the deliverables? Ha!

ERIK: Yes, it feels like we've made some progress and I'm looking forward to our next measurable objectives.

BRAD: Yeah, that's what I thought. That's what it looked like. Say, you guys need another beer?

PENNY: Not for me, but this was really good.

BRAD: Oh, yeah? That's great. That's Erik's. He said he wanted something dark, spicy and sweet. I should have warned you. Ha!

ERIK: (flustered) I... ugh.. well.. I like adventure.

PENNY: Exotics? Is that it?

ERIK: I've never wanted life to be bland.

LYNN: Well that's probably enough for today. Thank you, Erik. And Brad, it was a pleasure meeting you.

BRAD: I just hope you come back.

PENNY: Oh, we'll be back. Thank you. (Lynn and Penny exit)

ERIK: That was a good start, I think.

BRAD: Erik, I didn't know you were into hot black chicks?

ERIK: Neither did I until I met her.

BRAD: I mean, dude, I thought you were gay.

ERIK: I was. For a while. Then the feelings just shifted, changed. You know what I mean?

BRAD: No, I don't think so.

ERIK: Somebody like her comes a long and I think, now that's interesting!

BRAD: Ha! Whatever man. Anyway thanks for coming over to talk to them. I really appreciate your help.

ERIK: I'm enjoying it. Listen, let's catch up next week. Sound good?

BRAD: Any time, man. You know where I am. I'm here to make the beer! Ha!

Scene 2   two years have passed

Penny is sitting with Brad at the table in the taproom

PENNY: It looks like you are doing a really good job with the new brewing intern, Brad.

BRAD: Thanks. Ha! He's a good kid. Learning fast.

PENNY: Is he from the community college?

BRAD: One from my class, yeah. Get a taste off real brewing, instead of on a kitchen counter.

PENNY: But everybody starts somewhere.

BRAD: Ha! Yeah, that's right. I started in the kitchen, and look at me now!

PENNY: Brad, are you guys free tonight? I have somebody special that I'd like you to meet.

BRAD: Well it's date night tonight for me and Lynn, and she really likes to keep that to ourselves. Who is it? Who's coming?

PENNY: My son, Cornell.

BRAD: Really? I didn't know you had a son. How old?

PENNY: He's twenty three now. But he has been on a study program in Africa. I haven't seen him in a year. Since Erik's funeral.

BRAD: Oh yeah, I think I saw him there. Geez, it's the anniversary of Erik's, isn't it. God, can you believe it's been a year already?

PENNY: They say it takes a year to get over, but I still think about him every day.

BRAD: Penny, I never really understood, how he died.

PENNY: He put a belt around his neck and he strangled himself. I found him on the bed, blue.

BRAD: Oh my God. I'm so sorry. That's horrible. And why?

PENNY: I never understood. I still don't. It never made any sense. Not then, not now, a year later. We had one good year together. Happily married, I thought.

BRAD: And after what he did for me... I know I've probably said it before but having you guys buy me out was nearly the best thing that ever happened. And now you are the main owner. You are doing great.

PENNY: What was better?

BRAD: Meeting Lynn! Ha! She's great.

PENNY: Isn't your anniversary coming up?

BRAD: Last week. One year married, just before, you know, Erik. And I never thought it would happen to me. Just making beer, that's all I know about. But Lynn, you know, she knows everything. So smart. She's great.

PENNY: Yeah, she's great. Is she coming here?

BRAD: Uh-huh, she's going to pick me up in a few minutes.

PENNY: Brad, tell her to come in. I'd love to see her. (her phone buzzes) Excuse me.

BRAD: Yeah, right. OK. I'll tell her. See you later. (exits)

PENNY: (on call) Cornell? Is that you? Hey baby. Where are you?

(listens) Yeah, no. You're in the right place. That's right. Just come up the stairs and through the door. OK. Right. (hangs up)

(CORNELL enters, he is a handsome black man, with stylish, casual clothes. He looks fit and happy.)

(AIDA enters with Cornell, they are holding hands. She is an attractive black woman in her early 20s)

PENNY: (gets up and hugs them both) Son! It's so good to see you. And you are Aida? Welcome. Sit down.

AIDA: Thank you. It is wonderful to finally meet you in person.

PENNY: All this online business. It's not like the real thing. And I love your hair!

AIDA: Oh, you're sweet. Thank you.

CORNELL: How are you, Mama?

PENNY: I'm.. OK. I'm OK. Thanks for asking. But how are you two? How was the trip?

CORNELL: Good to be back.

PENNY: Brad, Brad, come meet my son.

BRAD: (comes to the table) Oh, hey. You're Cornell. I've heard a lot about you. Glad you're here. I'll get us some drinks. (exits)

PENNY: So, how was the trip?

AIDA: Long, hot, crowded. I'm just glad we're on the ground.

CORNELL: It's not Atlanta but Raleigh is nice.

PENNY: So what's the plan? Are you two getting married?

CORNELL: Whoa! Whoa! Mom, relax. We just sat down. There is something else I want to talk to you about.

PENNY: A baby?! Tell me it's a baby!

CORNELL: No, mom! It's not a baby. It's a business thing, I want to talk to you about. With Aida.

PENNY: Oh, now, humor me and just tell me you are going to get married. Just for me.

AIDA: We haven't put anything on the calendar yet but...

PENNY: See, Cornell. That's how you keep mama happy. Now what is the business thing?

LYNN: (arrives carrying drinks) Here you go, folks. Brad sent me over.

PENNY: Brad has you working here already?

LYNN: Heh! Just for you, Penny.

PENNY: Here sit down. I want you to meet my son, Cornell.

BRAD: (appears, sits down too) Say, Penny said you are doing some international thing. What's that all about?

CORNELL: I am doing an international study for my business degree. I've been in Ethiopia for a year. That's where I met Aida.

BRAD: That's great! Good for you. How do you like it? Africa.

CORNELL: Mostly we stay around the capital, but we've been able to travel and see some of the country too. So beautiful. So diverse. Arid desert. Highland pastures., Mountains down the middle. It's another world.

LYNN: Wow, that sounds amazing. And Aida, is it? Are you from there?

AIDA: No, I am from Maryland. My father was from Ethiopia.

PENNY: Was he fleeing the famine?

AIDA: He was a banker and there was a civil war. He got a job with the World Bank in DC. That's where he met my mother.

BRAD: Isn't it still civil war? I saw a movie about those pirates who attack tanker ships. I think Tom Hanks was in it. Did you see that?

CORNELL: Those are Somalis.

BRAD: Oh.

AIDA: It's like the difference between Sweden and Italy. They are very different. Ethiopia is peaceful and growing quickly now.

CORNELL: That's what I wanted to talk to you about. We have an idea for a development project and I wanted to run it by you.

PENNY: Tell me about it.

AIDA: Well, one of the greatest challenges for development of the country is for economic opportunity for women. We want to use a business model that allows women to be their own boss. Make their own money.

PENNY: That sounds fine and dandy. What do you have in mind?

CORNELL: We are thinking that, with some backing... we can develop a system where women can come in the morning to collect goods to sell and then go out with bicycle carts to sell their goods during the day. We provide credit for the goods, and they pay it back the next day and keep the profit.

PENNY: But what are they going to sell?

CORNELL: That's one of the issues. If it is something like jewelry, they are vulnerable to robbery. If it is something like melons, they would need a truck-load to make any money.

AIDA: We wanted to talk to you about it and ask you what you suggest.

PENNY: I don't know anything about the market in Ethiopia.

BRAD: Beer.

PENNY: Beer?

BRAD: The ladies. They could sell beer.

CORNELL: Beer?

BRAD: Sure. One woman with a bicycle could easily roll around with a 5 gallon keg, maybe a chunk of dried ice to keep it cold. She could roll up to a construction site and sell the whole thing in about an hour at the end of the day to the construction guys. Beer is a hell of a motivator for a working man. Especially convenient, cold beer. Ha!

AIDA: That's really interesting. The women could come and pick up the tanks as many times as they wanted.

PENNY: They could even hire people to go get kegs and return them, like runners. And, they are kegs. We don't call them tanks.

AIDA: Sorry.

LYNN: And you could sponsor music events too. Sell the beer there. You'd be supporting the arts.

CORNELL: The hip-hop arts...

BRAD: As long as they buy beer who cares what the music is. And don't they have pretty cool music there too in Africa? That sounds like fun. Music and beer. Who doesn't like that?

AIDA: The Muslims. They don't drink alcohol.

BRAD: OK, so don't invite them. Or invite them and maybe they get a taste of a great beer and see the light.

AIDA: I don't think that's how it would go.

CORNELL: Anyway, that's a really interesting idea. Using beer.

AIDA: I have some uncles who could help us with warehouses, trucks, workers, that sort of thing.

PENNY: And how much of this backing is all this going to cost?

AIDA: A hundred thousand dollars would probably get everything going.

PENNY: A hundred? I would consider fifty.

CORNELL: We could sell your beer...

BRAD: Yeah, hey!

PENNY: Brad, we're not set up to export beer. It would make more sense to brew it there. Beer is 95% water you know. And heavy.

BRAD: I could set up a brewery there. Make it locally, train some young guys how to brew Bad Penny.

CORNELL: Bad Penny?

PENNY: (lifts her glass) Our brown ale. That's what Erik called it when we took over the brewery. He renamed the brewery Big Boss and renamed the beer Bad Penny. Put my picture on the label. It is our most popular beer among black women.

LYNN: How would you say Big Boss Beer in Ethiopian?

AIDA: Big Boss Beer. We would do it in English.

PENNY: OK, let me think on it. Let's put it to bed for the night and go get some dinner. I'm starved.

BRAD: You guys go ahead. Me and Lynn, we're going to get a pizza up by our house. I'll see you in the morning.

LYNN: Great to see you Penny. And nice to meet you too.

(all exit)

Scene 3 two weeks have gone by, for Cornell and Aida's visit

Brad and Penny in the tap room

PENNY: (looking over papers) Sales are up, Brad. We're doing well.

BRAD: Yeah, making a lot of beer.

PENNY: That promotion for your new one really went well.

BRAD: Yeah, we're pretty much maxed out right now. We should start to plan for some new tanks. Especially if we're going to be sending beer to Cornell and Aida.

PENNY: I wanted to talk to you about that.

BRAD: Yeah?

PENNY: Do you know Fred Matt at Saranac? They make Utica Club.

BRAD: Yeah, I met him one time. Nice guy.

PENNY: Well, I met Fred when we were both in graduate school, doing our MBAs. I called him up to talk about this export idea. Fred says they have capacity at their brewery. They could make our beer there and ship it to Cornell. I'm thinking that you should go visit and see if it will work.

BRAD: Have Utica Club make Bad Penny? I guess but I mean, I don't know.

PENNY: Remember it was your idea. You told them they should sell beer. Do you want to see your idea work out?

BRAD: Sure. I mean, I'll go wherever you want. I'll go to Ethiopia.

PENNY: Well, soon, maybe but one thing at a time. Listen Cornell and Aida are coming to say goodbye. They are going back to get things going.

BRAD: Right. Wow. I think it is going to be fun. Making beer in Africa...

PENNY: Here they are now.

CORNELL: (enters) Hey Mom.

AIDA: Good morning, Mrs. Prince.

PENNY: Please, call me Penny. Now sit down and tell me what the plan is.

(all sit, Brad exits)

AIDA: So the next steps are to begin talking to women about the project. Then bank accounts.

PENNY: Send me the details when you have them and I can wire you some money.

CORNELL: Right. And I like the music sponsorship idea, to have a concert and selling beer. And the women can make some good money right from the start.

PENNY: Well you two. I love you and I'm willing to help. But remember, if things are not going well, do not hide it from me. Just tell me and we'll decide what to do. Now go. Go change the world.

CORNELL: Yes, mom.

AIDA: Thank you, Penny.

PENNY: Go. Change the world.

(Cornell and Aida exit, Penny is alone at the table)

(end)

Over Needles

By Rick Regan

The story is about a flight from California to Las Vegas that gets remote-controlled into landing at Needles, California air strip. Some men come on the plane to carry off one of the passengers.

Characters:

CAPTAIN	Captain of the airplane
HELEN	Chief Steward
ORVILLE	passenger and blogger about the gold market
WENDY	wife of ORVILLE
TOWER	various flight controllers at the airports
FED1	man with badge, leader of the group of men on the ground

September 10, 2020

Players:

CAPTAIN:	Ed Backes
HELEN:	Lyn Peticolas
ORVILLE:	BT McNichol
WENDY:	JC Glanville
TOWER:	Maura Vincent
FED1:	Rick Regan

Scene: Interior of commuter commercial airplane, loading passengers

HELEN: (head flight attendant)

Thank you for joining us today, ladies and gentlemen. Once everything is stowed and everyone is seated, we'll close the cabin doors and begin our flight.

WENDY: Can you put this up above for me hon'?

ORVILLE: Can you give me a minute, here? I'm trying to get down the aisle and now I have you breathing down my neck.

WENDY: Oh sure, take your time. It's not like the whole plane is waiting for you behind me. No, they have plenty of time to watch you fold your jacket. Is your newspaper creased and folded right too?

ORVILLE: OK, Ok. Give me your bag. There. Are you happy now? Can we just sit down and buckle up. I don't feel so good. You know I hate flying. Especially when we are flying to visit your mother.

WENDY: You sit by the window. So if you fall asleep you won't be leaning on me and breathing all over me!

(people are seated, Helen closes the door)

HELEN: (on microphone) Thank you ladies and gentlemen. We are glad to welcome you on board today for our Canada Air flight 301, departing today from sunny Orange County, John Wayne Airport. Our destinations today will be Las Vegas, Nevada; Flagstaff, Arizona; Las Cruses, New Mexico; up to Amarillo, Texas; then swinging north to Wichita, Kansas; Lincoln, Nebraska; then a long stretch up I-29 to Fargo, North Dakota; and finally back home for our crew based in Winnipeg, Manitoba, Canada.

Now sit back and relax as we enjoy the ride in this Canadian-built Bombardier Business Jet. We will prepare for take off.

CAPTAIN: Good afternoon, ladies and gentlemen. This is the captain speaking. We sure are glad to have you fly with us at Canadian Air today. Please take a moment to notice the exits and follow all of the instructions of Chief Steward Helen and her award-winning flight crew. We should have a pleasant ride today. Looks like smooth flying all the way to Manitoba. Now sit back and enjoy the ride.

ORVILLE: Geez, can we get on with it already?

WENDY: And how about some air?

ORVILLE: I'm sweating like I've been drugged. I am going to be drenched by the time we get to your mother's.

WENDY: I know, right. By the time we get to Fargo I'm going to feel like a basketball. Going up and down, you know. Like a basketball.

ORVILLE: Geez, why did we sign up for this puddle jumper? You know how my nerves are. Eight take-offs and landings before we get out of this flying egg carton? Just to save a couple of nickels.

WENDY: Tom, do you know how hard it is to find a flight from California to North Dakota? It's a good thing we made this flight or we would have waited another sixteen hours for the next one.

ORVILLE: It's going to take sixteen hours just to get to Fargo. Oh doctor!

WENDY: Listen, just settle yourself. Once we're in the air you can look out at the scenery. You know that relaxes you.

ORVILLE: What relaxes me is sitting at my desk in front of my keyboard. I write and think, and slowly the world changes.

WENDY: The world doesn't change because of your writing. You pen a blog about the gold and silver markets. That's not going to change the world.

ORVILLE: You think my work is not important? You think I'm wasting my time telling investors the truth about the fraud in the gold market? It's how I make a living. You know that.

WENDY: I know that you have been banging the drum for your "subscribers" that there is some deep-seated conspiracy and, any minute now!, you are going to blow the lid off the whole thing. I can't believe there are so many dupes and rubes that would pay you for your opinion on the gold market. What a racket!

ORVILLE: But the cover is almost blown. In two weeks the whole thing is going to come crashing down! They don't have enough gold in London to cover their positions...

WENDY: Save your breath. I've heard it a million times. "The gold market is manipulated." "The bullion banks are a fraud." And on and on. And, you know what, nothing has ever happened.

ORVILLE: I am shining the light. I am telling the truth. I am providing real and valuable insight to my subscribers.

WENDY: Your ignoramuses with no common sense, you mean.

ORVILLE: Oh, why bother... I'm going to get some sleep.

TOWER: (in the headset of the Captain)

            CANADA 301, this is the tower. You ready to roll?

CAPTAIN: (in the headset, to the Tower controller)

Tower, CANADA 301 here, ready to roll.

TOWER: Very good, CANADA 301. Take a position behind AGEAN 48 Heavy, in the blue and white. Then easy out and churn and burn.

CAPTAIN: Roger that, Tower. CANADA 301 out behind AGEAN 48 Heavy. We'll give him plenty of room and then it's up and out.

TOWER: 10-4 CANADA 301. Thanks for visiting Orange County and have a safe flight today.

CAPTAIN: (over the cabin intercom) Ladies and gentlemen, buckle up because we are lined up for take off. We'll be in the air shortly.

WENDY: It smells like gas. Is it supposed to smell like gas? Maybe the plane is leaking. (rings flight call button) Excuse me!

HELEN: (comes down the aisle) What's the matter here?

WENDY: It smells like gas. Is the plane broken?

HELEN: No, the plane is not broken. The tower has us lined up behind a very large jet. Sometimes when they are waiting to take off, there is a strong smell of aviation fuel. It will go away once we are away from the big plane.

ORVILLE: I wish *I* was on the big plane.

HELEN: Now just relax. We'll be in the air shortly.

WENDY: It just stinks. That's all.

CAPTAIN: (through intercom) OK folks. Here we go.

(engines roar and airplane takes off)

CAPTAIN: (to Tower) Tower this is CANADA 301. We are clear and heading to Las Vegas.

TOWER: Very good, CANADA 301. Proceed to twenty thousand feet and I will hand you off to flight control LAS.

CAPTAIN: Thank you, John Wayne. See you next time. CANADA 301 out.

HELEN: (into flight intercom, to the Captain) Captain, when we reach cruising altitude, is there anything I can get you? A coffee or snack?

CAPTAIN: Thank you, Chief Helen. A coffee would be nice. I will ring the chime in a moment.

HELEN: Very good, Captain.

HELEN: (into the cabin intercom) Ladies and gentlemen, in a moment the captain will ring the bell indicating that we have reached cruising altitude. It will be safe to move about the cabin and I will be offering a selection of beverages and snacks.

(cabin bell: Bong!)

ORVILLE: What happened to flying? It used to be glamorous. Dinner served with linen napkins and fine china. Now it's plastic wrapped cookies and coffee out of a rubber bladder.

WENDY: When were you ever on a flight with real china plates? You haven't left Burbank in twenty years.

ORVILLE: In my college years, you know. I travelled. I saw things.

WENDY: I bet you've never seen the inside of a jumbo jet. Like a 747. They say they used to have a cocktail lounge in the upstairs of the 747. That's what was in the hump, you know on the top.

ORVILLE: Yes, I know what a 747 is. When gold is transferred from the refiners in Switzerland to the vaults in New York, they use a especially outfitted Boeing 747. No passengers. Just the elite flight crew and the gold bars.

WENDY: What happens if the hit turbulence? Do the bars just get jumbled up and fall all over the place? And how do they keep the crew from sliding a few bars into a paper sack? Nobody would know.

ORVILLE: Of course they'd know. The gold people have an inventory number for every single bar. That, and the crew gets weighed before and after each flight. It's foolproof!

WENDY: I bet. Maybe a guy walks onto the scale and he's already got two red bricks in his pocket. Did you ever think of that?

ORVILLE: Of course they have thought of that. They have thought of everything.

WENDY: Sure, sure.

(cabin bell: Bing-Bong!)

HELEN: (phone to captain) Yes, Captain?

CAPTAIN: I'd take some of that coffee if you have some fresh.

HELEN: Right away, sir.

(Helen prepares the coffee and knocks on the cockpit door. The door opens and Helen goes in, closing the door behind her.)

HELEN: Here you are. Nice and fresh.

CAPTAIN: Thank you, Helen. Say, tell me, how did you get stuck on this milk run? I thought your seniority would have you on the trans-Atlantics or Toronto-Cuba.

HELEN: Captain, well, you know how the schedule works. I'm trying to get back to Ottawa, if I can jump-seat from Winnipeg. How about you? You're awfully senior to be hot-stopping in Wichita.

CAPTAIN: I just got back from Hawaii for two weeks with my kids. Now back in the rotation at the bottom of the stack, just like a junior rookie. It's alright. Lot of good flying on this run.

HELEN: Captain, excuse me, but isn't it too early to be descending?

CAPTAIN: What the...? We are descending and turning. This is not in the flight plan. The controls are not responding. I have switched the autopilot off but I can't control the plane.

HELEN: Could somebody remote control us?

CAPTAIN: Not that I have ever heard of. You go back and prepare for landing. I will contact flight control Las Vegas.

HELEN: (intercom) Ladies and gentlemen, the captain has asked that everyone remain seated and he is turning the seat belt light on. Please remain seated.

WENDY: What's going on? Are we going to crash?

ORVILLE: We just took off. That's when the accidents always happen, taking off or landing.

WENDY: Orville I want to tell you something, before... you know. Orville, I have always loved you.

ORVILLE: But? Is there a but? You have loved me, but...?

WENDY: No buts, Orville. That's all.

ORVILLE: Oh, ok. Sure. I love you too. So there.

CAPTAIN: (microphone to Las Vegas air control) L-A-S this is CANADA 301.

TOWER: CANADA 301, this is McCarran Tower. Go ahead.

CAPTAIN: Tower, I have to declare an emergency. I have lost control of the airplane.

TOWER: 301 I have you on the screen and all systems report normal. You are making a smooth descent, on approach to Needles Field.

CAPTAIN: Tower, I am not flying the plane. Nobody is. The autopilot is off.

TOWER: 301 It looks like an angel is flying with you then because you are on course for a smooth landing into Needles Field.

CAPTAIN: Tower, we are lined up and almost at touchdown. I am not flying the plane.

(Plane lands, tires screech, engines wind down, flaps deploy)

CAPTAIN: (over cabin intercom) Ladies and gentlemen, it looks like we didn't have our paperwork all lined up and air traffic asked us to make a quick stop off here in Needles. Please remain seated while we get this sorted out.

(a big black SUV roars up outside the plane)

ORVILLE: Needles? Is that one of their stops? I don't even see any other planes.

WENDY: Who knows? If they stop in Las Cruses maybe they stop in Needles. But who would want to stop here?

TOWER: (into CAPTAIN's headset) CANADA 301, this is ground control Needles Field. Do you copy?

CAPTAIN: 10-4 Tower. What is the meaning of this?

TOWER: CANADA 301, we have a report of a potential terrorist on board your aircraft. We have reason to believe he is a danger to all souls aboard.

CAPTAIN: A terrorist?

TOWER: That's correct, 301. We are going to wheel out a ramp and a few of our fellows will come in to apprehend the suspect.

CAPTAIN: Negative, Tower. This is a Canadian plane. I will not allow an unauthorized entry. This is Canadian property.

TOWER: 301, you are on U.S. soil, *amigo*. Just open the door. We'll have you back in the air in under 10-minutes.

(cabin bell, Bing-Bong!)

HELEN: (phone to captain) Yes, captain?

CAPTAIN: Helen, there are some men who want to apprehend one of the passengers. They say he is a suspected terrorist. Do you see anybody who looks like a terrorist?

HELEN: No, Captain. Just a bunch of regular people.

CAPTAIN: Helen, they will approach the door but do not open the door. Only open the door on my orders.

HELEN: Yes, captain.

(man bangs on the side of the door, showing some kind of badge)

WENDY: What's going on? Who are these people?

          (man bangs on the door again.)

HELEN: (opens the door) Who are you?

          (three men come in, they go past Helen and straight to Orville)

FED1:   You a one, Orville McGuinn?

ORVILLE: Yes. Who are you?

WENDY: What do you want with my husband?

FED1:   You are coming with us.

ORVILLE: Why? What for? What are the charges?

FED1:   We're not the police, Mr. McGuinn. Come with us.

          (one of the men cuts, Wendy's seatbelt and lifts her out of the seat)

          (the other man reaches Orville's seatbelt, unbuckles it and grabs Orville by the shirt, dragging him into the aisle)

ORVILLE: (being dragged to the front) What is this about?! Who sent you?! This is about the gold, isn't it?! Isn't it?!

WENDY: Honey!! Orville! Let him go! Let my husband go!

          (Wendy is restrained by one of the men, she struggles against him)

ORVILLE: You don't really have it?! Do you?! You DIRTY BASTARDS!! You never had it! Not in England! Not in New York! They are probably selling red bricks wrapped in gold foil! I knew it! I knew it!

FED1:   Shut up! You are coming with us.

          (Orville is dragged out of the front of the plane)

          (Captain opens the cockpit door to see the men dragging Orville away)

WENDY: I'm going with him! If you are taking him, I'm going too. You have to take me too.

HELEN: (to Wendy, whispers) Madam, he's not coming back. If you go with him, you will be dead too.

WENDY: Aaaaggghhh!! Or-VILLE!

          (Helen holds her back)

CAPTAIN: What the hell is going on? You can't come in here! Release that man, immediately!

FED1:   (to Helen, quietly) *Render unto Caesar.*

HELEN: (to Fed1, quietly) *Render unto Caesar.*

CAPTAIN: I am the Captain of this ship!

(Captain, grabs the man holding Orville, on the platform just outside the door)

(Captain, pulls out an automatic pistol, puts it to the man's head)

CAPTAIN: Unhand him. Now!

(man lets go of Orville.)

ORVILLE: Oh, my God!

CAPTAIN: Return to your seat!

ORVILLE: Yes, sir. Right away sir. Yes, sir!

(Orville goes down the aisle)

WENDY: Orville!

ORVILLE: Wendy, we have to sit down immediately! The captain said we have to sit down. We have to sit down! Sit down, Wendy!

CAPTAIN: (to the man with the gun at his head)

Now you listen to me. I am going to let you go and we are going to close this door. Then we are going to fly away. Do you understand?

FED1:   It's not worth all of this, Captain. We'll just catch him someplace else. That's all. This was just a convenient and safe way to put our hands on him.

CAPTAIN: Who are you people? FBI?

FED1:   Not exactly. More like the Justice League. You know, from the comic books. Now can you put the gun down?

CAPTAIN: Are you going to let us fly away? How did you get us here?

FED1:   It's something we learned to do in I-raq, take control of the autopilot remotely. It is very handy. Yeah, sure. Just put the gun down and we won't bother you. Fly away. Sorry for the inconvenience. I just thought we had the way paved already.

(FED1 looks at Helen)

CAPTAIN: Are you part of the government, the military?

FED1:   Indirectly. That's all I can say.

CAPTAIN: Helen, are you in on this? Are you part of their plan?

HELEN: Captain, I work for Canadian Airlines. You know that. I don't know anything about this.

(Captain, swings his gun and pushes it against Helen's forehead)

CAPTAIN: You had better tell me the truth. What's going on, Helen?

FED1: It's like she said, she didn't know this was going to happen. She's as innocent as you are, aren't you Helen?

HELEN: Captain, put the gun down. Let's continue our flight and get these people to their homes. Put the gun down and get back into the cockpit. These men will not interfere in our flight.

CAPTAIN: (lowers the gun) Who are you?

HELEN: Get into the cockpit. Start the engines. Let's go.

(Helen closes the door on the man on the platform. The engines start up again. The plane starts rolling for takeoff.)

CAPTAIN: (intercom) Prepare for takeoff.

HELEN: (intercom) Ladies and gentlemen, please buckle yourselves in and prepare for takeoff. When we get to cruising altitude, I will continue our beverage service before we arrive in Las Vegas.

(Engines roar, plane takes off)

WENDY: Orville, I was so worried about you. The woman said they would kill me if I went along with you.

ORVILLE: Those men wanted to kill me. They want to silence my voice. But I'm right. The whole thing is about to explode! The whole global economy is going to self-destruct, right in front of our eyes.

WENDY: Why would they want to kill you, Orville?

ORVILLE: Because I have exposed very powerful people as being corrupt and, worse, broke! They want to keep the circus going but I am speaking the truth.

WENDY: But will they be there when we get to Las Vegas? Or Las Cruses? Or Wichita? They will hunt us down!

ORVILLE: We've got to have a plan! We've got to be invisible, disappear.

HELEN: (appearing in the aisle) I brought you both some water, or coffee if you like. I'm so sorry for the misunderstanding. They said it was a medical emergency.

WENDY: (drinking the water) Oh thank God. What were they going to do to him?

ORVILLE: (drinking the water) Kill me, that's what!

HELEN: Oh, no. Probably ask a few questions. Surely it was a mistake. I've never had that happen before. It was so sudden. Now try to get some sleep. We'll be in Las Vegas before you know it.

ORVILLE: It must be the shock but I just want to go to sleep. Wendy, move over... Are you asleep already? Wendy?

HELEN: She's just sleeping

ORVILLE: (to Helen) Wait, you did this. (looks at the water) You did this! It was you!

(Orville slumps down in seat)

HELEN: You folks just rest up. We'll be on the ground soon.

(Helen goes back to the front)

HELEN: (intercom) Ladies and gentlemen, please prepare for landing. We will be touching down in Las Vegas in a few moments.

(cabin bell: Bing-bong!)

HELEN: (cockpit intercom) Captain, all set for landing.

CAPTAIN: Helen, I want some straight answers when we get on the ground.

HELEN: Yes, Captain. And, sir, one more thing. We may need medical services when we land. It appears that two of the passengers have become ill.

CAPTAIN: Is it serious?

HELEN: I'm afraid so, sir.

(end)

Win a dinner with Alan Greenspan!

By Rick Regan, August 26, 2020

The story is about a man, Willie, who wins a dinner with former Fed Chair Alan Greenspan. Willie wants to understand why he is poor and other people are rich.

Characters:

Alan Greenspan

      former chairman of the Federal Reserve Bank of the United States of America

Willie   poor man from rural North Carolina

Waiter   restaurant waiter

Note:

This was not performed in this version.

A similar version by Ed Backes was used.

Scene: fancy restaurant in fancy hotel in DC

ALAN: (sitting alone, reading his phone. Clear cocktail on the table.)

WAITER: (directs a man to the table) Ahem.

WILLIE: You mister Greenspan?

ALAN: Yes. Who are you?

WILLIE: Hello, sir. I'm Willie. I won that there con-test to have dinner with you.

ALAN: Umm. I think there has been a mistake.

WILLIE: No mistake. I got all the I's dotted and T's crossed. Fair'n square.

ALAN: Excuse me. (Picks up phone. Dials. Talks into phone.) James, listen.. oh, yes. No he's here. I see. Really? Tonight? It wasn't on my schedule. Make sure I am not surprised by these things. OK. (hangs up)

WILLIE: See? All right.

ALAN: It appears I am to have the pleasure of your company tonight. I have another engagement in forty-five minutes but I can give you my attention until then. What can he get you?

WILLIE: Oh, well. Whatever you're having, sir.

ALAN: Walter, two gin martini's, please. One for me and one for him. We'll look at the menu in a moment.

WAITER: Very good sir.

ALAN: So, Willie. Please sit down. Tell me about yourself.

WILLIE: I'm Willie. Everybody calls me Willie. At the plant, the chicken plant, everybody say, "Hey, Willie! Hey, Willie! Bring mo' ice!"

ALAN: Ice?

WILLIE: I hauls ice at the Per-due plant. Near outside Ahoskie. Best ice hauler anywhere, I bet!

ALAN: I see. And what do you want from me?

WILLIE: Well, Mister Greenspan, I figure you 'bout the only man in the whole wide world who know how everything work. Everything. The money. The government. Wars and peace. Even the aliens, they probably told you. I don't expect you care 'bout Elvis, but maybe I ask anyway. And about slaves and reparations. Ev'thing!

ALAN: I'm sorry Willie. I don't know about any of those things. I study monetary policy.

WILLIE: Well, that's just it. That's what I want to know about. Monetary policy.

ALAN: Why is that?

WILLIE: Mister Greenspan, I never had no money in my life. No real money. I had an uncle. He had a bank and he tell me, "Willie, you got to save yo' moneys. You got to stack it up. Then for long it be stacking up itself." Well I never understood. How could moneys stack itself?

ALAN: Compounding interest. I expect that is what he meant.

WILLIE: Compound int'rest? Is that like a compound bow, get stronger the more you pull it?

ALAN: A.. Compound bow? What is that?

WILLIE: For hunting, sir. Like for wild hogs. You know, when they gets in the yard. Don't want to use no bullets cause they children 'round. But a compound bow and a arrow, thunk! Right behind the ear. Dead, on time. And good eating. Speaking of eating...

ALAN: Of course. Walter, could you take our orders?

WAITER: Yes, of course, Mister Greenspan. What can I get you tonight?

ALAN: I will have my usual Greek salad, with a few extra olives, and a cup of the onion soup. How is the feta tonight?

WAITER: Wonderful, sir. Our cheese monger has the feta under very close watch, especially for you, sir.

ALAN: Willie, is there anything you'd like? Fish, or chicken? A steak?

WILLIE: Oh, no, I can't eat no chicken. Not for a long time. I handle them chickens twelve hour a day. Live chicken, dead chicken, sick chicken, cut up chicken. I bring the ice, but I can't eat 'em.

ALAN: I see. Is there anything else that comes to mind. The chef here is quite remarkable.

WILLIE: Now I am real partial to ham hocks and greens.

ALAN: Understandably. Walter, what do you think?

WAITER: I will ask the chef but I am confident that we can accommodate. Anything for dessert?

ALAN: Perhaps a sherry at the time. Willie?

WILLIE: You wouldn't have a slice of coconut crème pie left to the side, would you? I love that pie.

WAITER: I will defer to the pastry chef but I am sure she will have a few ideas. Very good gentlemen.

WILLIE: Now Mister Greenspan, I want to know, need to know, how come they poor people and they rich people? I been poor my whole life. Everybody I know be poor. Except the man who runs the plant, from the Per-due company. He live up in Norfolk and drive down everyday. I never been to his house but I bet it real nice. He seem like a real nice man. But I don't understand why he rich and everybody, all around, poor as mice.

ALAN: Well, Willie, my work, my research, centers around the market function where an individual or a company exploits their own hard work and innovation for advantage and wealth creation.

WILLIE: What's that mean?

ALAN: OK. You trade your time and effort, and they pay you, give you money. Right.

WILLIE: Sure enough.

ALAN: So your contribution to the company is the sum of your time - and your effort, hauling ice, correct?

WILLIE: Yes, sir.

ALAN: So the company adds up your time and your ice-hauling and pays you. And you value the money, so you keep going to work.

WILLIE: But why is he rich and I not? He works hard. I work hard. Only twenty-four hours in the day. It ain't like he got more hours. But he must make a whole lot more than me.

ALAN: I assume that the plant manager is doing more than just... just hauling ice, Willie. He's responsible for the smooth running of the plant. That is more valuable than hauling ice. And surely there must be a machine to move ice around, a conveyor or something, to deliver ice.

WILLIE: But I'm the best ice hauler all around! Ain't no machine haul ice like me.

ALAN: What happens when you go home at night? Do they turn off the machines and close the factory, all because you are gone home so nobody has any ice?

WILLIE: They's two other fellas haul ice when I'm out.

ALAN: But you are the main one, hauling ice.

WILLIE: Right.

ALAN: And how long until you retire, do you think?

WILLIE: Retire? Can't afford retire. Can't afford the doctor-man. Can't afford the rent. Can't afford put gas up my car. It's like them po-lice cuffs; if you squeeze 'em, they get tighter. Ain't never get looser. It's like that all the time.

ALAN: Well that's how the economy works.

WILLIE: But does it have to work like that? Does it have to be that the Per-due man work hard and makes a lot of money. I work hard and I get near to nothing. They care about them chickens more than me. Does it have to be like that? It seem like there's a whole lot of money in the world, but folks don't want to spread it around and help out poor folks.

ALAN: Well, people leverage their advantages, natural or systemic. We have a very dynamic economy.

WILLIE: I don't understand. Explain that to me. Why some people got... natural... advantage?

ALAN: If a person grows up in a wealthy family, they will have the benefits of stable housing, good education, broad social support. But, economic data indicate that someone born into the lowest quartile, or poor, is going to remain poor throughout his life. That's how it is.

WILLIE: But I don't understand why them folks don't help everybody. Not just them that already got theirs. Why not help all the Americans?

ALAN: You mean just give people money? Direct-payments are a profound moral hazard.

WILLIE: Moral hazard? They gone pay the rent!

ALAN: Direct payments have been shown to de-incentivize work.

WILLIE: Mister Greenspan, I haul ice in a chicken plant. If I could make more money doing anything, anything else, I'd do it. Maybe if there was 'direct payments' to Americans, the Per-due company would pay us more - spending our lives hauling ice or working on the cut-up line.

ALAN: Wage hikes would negatively impact the operating costs of the corporation. The company would likely close the plant and find a location with lower labor costs.

WILLIE: Good! Let 'em move then. They make everybody sick, broken down working in that plant. They take all the water from the town and everything smells like raw chicken. I'd be glad to see them go if there was any way to not starve to death. Maybe with your 'di-rect payment' idea, we can spend time with our children, go to choich, help out with my mother. She by herself.

ALAN: You are talking about diverting tax dollars to fund free handouts. You know the old adage, that when something is taxed, there is less of it, but if something is free, the demand is unlimited. We can't just siphon off the GDP for handouts.

WILLIE: Why not? Other governments, other countries do it. Seems like this government don't care no how about nobody, 'cept rich folks.

ALAN: And corporations.

WILLIE: Xactly. Maybe we ought to tell people to leave, light-out. Go someplace where brotherly love is the law, not them handcuffs that only get tighter. Maybe it's time to make a plan to empty this country out. Just leave the rich folks and the Per-due company. The rich folks can have all the chicken they wantin'.

ALAN: A reverse migration of Americans is highly undesirable. By destabilizing the labor market, wages would... rise. And communities would be hollowed out, robbing the municipal tax base.

WILLIE: Oh, the municipality would be robbed? Or the town been robbin' the people all along, for the good of the Per-due company.

ALAN: It's just that the US has a flexible, dynamic economy, with stable institutions and rule of law. That can not be said about many places around the world.

WILLIE: You don't think that some welcoming country wouldn't be better off with a whole bunch of Americans, bringing their American dollars?

Hear now, the Per-due company want to 'annex' the next lot over from theirs. They say they need it for truck turn arounds. Maybe they do. But Mister Barney grows food on that lot, keeps hogs. You think the Per-due company gone pay him what it will cost him to up and move someplace else? Shoot no! They gone just take it; and throw a sack of pennies at him, that's all.

ALAN: To your point about American emigration, America remains the beacon to world's smartest and most innovative talent. The best and the brightest from all over the world can have more opportunity here to follow their dreams. That's why they still come here. For Americans to forsake that dynamism would be to forego our inherited legacy of progress and economic mobility.

WILLIE: Ain't nobody economically mobile or dynamically innovative in Ahoskie. Just poor folks, that can't get no help no how.

ALAN: Your pessimism about your opportunity for wealth creation is, frankly, disappointing. Investment opportunities abound, from real estate to equity exposure, small business entrepreneurship and revenue generating assets.

WILLIE: Oh, ok. If you already got a dollar, you could make another dollar. I see.

ALAN: Consider this, Willie. Think about a Coke machine. If you bought a Coke machine and put it in the plant, kept it stocked with sodas, that machine will make money for you all day and all night, while you are not even there. You stock it up, take out the money, and let it get back to work. That is using credit to purchase the asset which generates income. When the credit is paid off, everything is profit, 24 hours a day. But you will want to borrow more money to put in more machines, at more places in the plant, or maybe at other factories. That's how you grow.

WILLIE: But they already got Coke machines.

ALAN: Something else then. The point is that the economy provides opportunity, to grow. Not just handouts.

WILLIE: Mister Greenspan, I'm sure you right. You know all about these things. I just been poor my whole life and it don't seem like that's ever going to end. Coke machines or not.

ALAN: I can't give you a straight answer about what you are looking for. I'm sorry.

WILLIE: That's alright, Mister Greenspan. You did what you could. You did your best. I know you are busy so I'ma let you eat in peace.

WAITER: (appearing with dinners) Are you leaving, sir?

WILLIE: I best get on.

WAITER: I would be happy to wrap this to go for you.

WILLIE: Well, that would be real nice.

WAITER: Just a moment.

WILLIE: Mister Greenspan, thank you for taking your time to educate me. And I got to tell you... they wasn't no contest. I made that up for your man. He believed me and told me where you was. I just came over. But you real nice to me and I gone to tell folks that I had a real fine time talking about the whole world with Mister Greenspan.

WAITER: (appears with take-out) Here you go, sir.

ALAN: Willie, I don't know if I have the answers for what you want but consider this, in America there is generally opportunity for everybody, but sometimes not for you. That's how it goes.

WILLIE: It just get tighter, don't it.

ALAN: Yup.

WILLIE: Good night, sir. (exits)

ALAN: (begins eating his soup)

(END)

Hang 'em!

by Rick Regan

<u>Characters:</u>

John: Manager of political operations

Mark: political staffer

Matt: political staffer

The story concerns the political concerns about what should be the policy priorities of the incumbent US President, upon re-election.

Note:

This was not performed

Scene: office building, conference room. John is the manager. He is alone, sitting at a table reading his phone.

MARK: (pokes his head in the door)

            Hey, John. Can I grab you for a minute?

JOHN: Sure. What's up? Here sit down.

MARK: I was thinking about something and wanted to run it by you.

JOHN: OK. Shoot.

MARK: Well with the upcoming re-election, I was thinking about the next term.

JOHN: Yeah, me too. Hard to work out what the priorities should be. We've gotten so much done, I'm not sure how we take it to the next level – for the next four years.

MARK: Right. Well, we made a lot of progress on capital punishment. I was thinking that we take the next step on abortion.

JOHN: What do you mean?

MARK: Well, abortion is murder, right?

JOHN: Right. Abortion is murder.

MARK: And we just got capital punishment for murder approved in all fifty states.

JOHN: Yeah...

MARK: I think we have the opportunity to knit the two ideas together and really make some progress.

JOHN: How is that?

MARK: Capital punishment for any woman who has had an abortion.

JOHN: Interesting. Just across the board?

MARK: Well, abortion is murder.

JOHN: Right. Abortion is murder.

MARK: So we look at all the records of women who have had abortions and justice is finally served, for murder.

JOHN: Hang on. Let's loop Matt into this.

            (buzzes and intercom)

JOHN: Matt, can you come into the conference room for a minute? Got a thing we're trying to hash out.

MATTHEW: (through intercom) Sure. Let me finish this thing and I'll be right in.

JOHN: (through intercom) Great.

JOHN: Are you thinking about a campaign timeline?

MARK: Probably not a positive before the election.

JOHN: Hmmm. Right. May generate more negative energy than positive among the base.

MARK: Right.

MATTHEW: Hey, guys. What's up?

JOHN: You tell him.

MARK: OK. So thinking about the next term, I was kicking around the idea of capital punishment for abortion.

MATTHEW: Capital punishment?

MARK: Well, abortion is murder.

MATTHEW: True. Abortion is murder.

JOHN: So, thinking about the progress we made with capital punishment in all fifty states...

MATTHEW: I see where you're going with this. Murder is murder.

MARK: Right. Murder is murder, and the punishment for murder is death.

MATTHEW: I see. Hmmm... Maybe we could have a facility in, spitballing here, Utah? To process the punishments? Like, centralized.

JOHN: I see a moral hazard there. It would seem like a death camp or something.

MARK: Right, we're not NAZI's.

MATTHEW: Right. HA-ha-ah!

JOHN: Ah-ha-ha!

MARK: Heh! Heh! Right?

JOHN: Right.

MARK: No, I think transparency has to be the watchword. Like sunshine.

MATTHEW: I see. Ok, so state by state then?

JOHN: Right. And public.

MATTHEW: Trials? Public trials?

MARK: Executions. People have to see the punishment.

MATTHEW: Hmmm.. Like a public hanging.

MARK: Right. So people know it is actually happening. Not just on TV. Anybody can fake TV.

JOHN: Right! Ha-ha-ha!

MATTHEW: Yeah! Ha-ha-ha!

MARK: Heh-heh-heh! I know, right? Heh!

MATTHEW: So just so that I'm clear, you want to hang every woman who has had an abortion in America. Is that it?

MARK: Well, abortion is murder.

JOHN: Abortion is murder.

MATTHEW: And the law of the land is that murderers are sentenced to death.

JOHN: All 50 states.

MARK: And not just execution. There should be a requirement to display the body for some period of time. Maybe seven days?

JOHN: That would be transparent. No question of justice not being served. Crime. Punishment.

MATTHEW: Seven days, though. That's a lot to display a dead body. You thinking outside?

MARK: I don't know. I guess I was thinking, you know, like the Romans, to display the body of the criminals along public streets.

MATTHEW: Just, like, along Main Street, USA?

MARK: Yeah. In a row, I suppose.

MATTHEW: At eye level? Couldn't somebody just come up and take the body away?

JOHN: We could use aluminum poles. And elevate them.

MATTHEW: Interesting. Aluminum is recyclable.

MARK: I hadn't gone this far but maybe attach the body with, like, stainless steel screws. That way they won't rust if it is raining and they are reusable.

MATTHEW: Re-use and Re-cycle. I like it. Part of a Green initiative.

JOHN: Shows we are *woke* to the environment.

MATTHEW: But one thing. You want to hang the criminal, and *then* display the body? Why not combine the two? Make the display the capital punishment.

JOHN: Like the Romans? Hmmm.

MARK: Kill two birds with one stone.

MATTHEW: *Kill two birds*, Ha! Ha! I see what you did there.

JOHN: Heheheheh!

MARK: Oh! Right. Heh!

JOHN: So maybe use an X-shape? Or a T-shape?

MATTHEW: Something like that. Maybe we don't want to get too lost in the weeds of the specifics.

MARK: Yeah, maybe consult an expert or something.

JOHN: Are you stuck on hanging?

MARK: Well, no, but that is what comes to mind.

JOHN: Because I am going to call States Rights on this and say that some states may want to do it differently. Maybe one state doesn't have a lot of rope. Maybe some states have a pharma industry and want to use their drugs.

MATTHEW: Or an oil and gas state. They may want to burn them at the stake. I don't think we can specify.

MARK: Yeah, I see what you mean. And I guess the method doesn't really matter. I mean, abortion is murder.

JOHN: Right. Abortion is murder.

MATTHEW: Getting back to the public thing. Why not just have it on TV? Like a new CSPAN channel.

MARK: CSPAN8, The Ocho!

MATTHEW: The Ocho! Heh!

JOHN: Hehehehe! The Ocho.

MARK: Well that's funny but I think one of the key aspects is the transparency again. If it is on TV, even *The Ocho!*, it is subject to suspicion of being faked.

JOHN: Like a loop of last year?

MARK: Yeah, in a million ways. That's why, I think, the punishments have to be public. And local. I'm thinking at county courthouses. All across America.

MATTHEW: From sea to shining sea?

JOHN: Wait. Again, I am thinking this is a state-level issue. Not a county sheriff, Bull Connor kind of thing. This has to be driven by the legislatures.

MARK: Well we'll have the courts in lock step so I'm thinking we go for a Constitutional Amendment.

JOHN: An amendment?

MARK: Right. Transparency is the key. Like a bright clear arrow. Declare abortion is murder and that justice is only satisfied by capital punishment, publicly and for the body to be displayed.

MATTHEW: What if there was a sign on each post that had the name and specifics of the crime?

JOHN: As in, Here is Jane Doe, convicted of murder by abortion.

MARK: I like that.

MATTHEW: Crazy thought: what if it was an electronic sign so it could be updated with details of the crime. *Became pregnant at seventeen and decided a baby was inconvenient.*

JOHN: Or, *Raped by her uncle when she was 18.*

MATTHEW: Or 16.

JOHN: Or 15.

MATTHEW: Or 14.

MARK: Right. We could detail the crime.

MATTHEW: You know…. Again, just throwing it against the wall… We could have extra space at the bottom of the screen where we could sell advertising space.

JOHN: Better than that, or along with, we could let the family provide an obituary. Fill out the picture. Who wouldn't pay for that?

MARK: Right. Heh!

MATTHEW: *Ms. Doe was raped at 14 by her uncle Lou but, after her abortion, went on to finish her nursing degree and practiced as a school nurse faithfully for thirty-five years. Much beloved by her family, her husband Jack, their three children, and recently a first grandchild.*

MARK: That's gold!

JOHN: I like it.

MATTHEW: Or, *Ms. Doe was involved with a politician when she volunteered as a campaign staffer. When she became pregnant, she was told to make the baby, "go away".*

JOHN: A politician. Hee heheh!

MATTHEW: Heh-heh-heh!

MARK: That's funny.

JOHN: So we need a ratification strategy for all fifty states.

MATTHEW: Wait. One question: what are the boundaries of the crime? Anybody ever?

MARK: I was thinking retroactive to the start of the President's term.

JOHN: I like it for practical reasons but I'm not sure if it would pass muster with the Supreme Court. It seems like an arbitrary starting point.

MATTHEW: Ok. Let's go back to Roe v. Wade. Any woman who voluntarily sought an abortion, legally at the time, would be liable for murder conviction now.

JOHN: That's interesting. Since it was legal there would be a definitive starting point. I like it.

MARK: And since there would be medical records of the events, then legal, we should be able to identify every abortion in the country from that point forward.

JOHN: My god, just think of all the murders.

MARK: Makes me sick. That's why I was thinking about extending our progress on murder to finally seek justice for the unborn. By hanging.

JOHN: Still stuck on the hanging. Listen, maybe we pitch it as hanging to make the images real but we'll have to compromise once we get down to brass tacks.

MATTHEW: And I don't love the public display thing. I still think it would be a lot more efficient on TV.

MARK: No. See the *public* punishment is the *public* demonstration of justice for the unborn. The system is fair, transparent and equal. Justice requires transparency all the way along. Don't you agree? I mean, abortion is murder.

JOHN: He's right. Abortion is murder.

MATTHEW: Abortion is murder.

MARK: So the punishment, by hanging or otherwise, requires the public display.

MATTHEW: I like the aluminum T-shape idea. We could prototype that for trials.

JOHN: Speaking of trials, won't we need to litigate and have trials for all of the criminals?

MARK: I don't think so. If we have the medical records, it will show that the person voluntarily committed murder of the unborn. We will have the details of the crime. No need for a trial.

MATTHEW: Is that transparent though? Just showing medical records isn't enough for a judge or jury.

MARK: It will be if we tell them it will be. We own the court so we can just tell them they are guilty.

JOHN:	I guess that's true. And if we have an amendment, that's pretty powerful too.
MATTHEW:	Do you think we can get three fourth of the states? That's thirty-eight states. To ratify?
JOHN:	I think with strong leadership from the top, grassroots pressure from the bottom, and some effective lobbying, we could get just about anything ratified.
MARK:	And it's not like this is a radical idea. You know? I mean, come on.
MATTHEW:	Yeah, I see what you mean. What kind of numbers are you looking at?
MARK:	Like criminal stats?
MATTHEW:	Yeah. How many women in the US have had abortions?
MARK:	The study I looked at, from 2017, said that one in four women will have had an abortion by the time she is forty-five.
JOHN:	So with, say three hundred million Americans, half would be women for one hundred and fifty million women. A quarter of that, thirty seven, call it forty, million women we'd be talking about.
MARK:	Right.
MATTHEW:	That's a lot of women.
MARK:	Right. That's why we need the amendment. To be sure that justice is served equally in America for the murdered unborn.
MATTHEW:	I see.
JOHN:	What about an enforcement arm? Do we leave it to the states or is this a job for the FBI? Do we need a new agency?
MATTHEW:	I think you are back to a states' rights issue. Won't each state have to handle it with their own resources? Wouldn't a governor put up opposition to a federal force coming in to prosecute a quarter of the women in the state?
MARK:	Execute. To execute a quarter of the women in the state.
JOHN:	I see what you mean. National Guard maybe? Well, let's table that for the moment. We don't want to get too far off in the weeds.
MARK:	Re-visiting the agenda for the next four years, I was wondering if we want to raise the three-fifths-of-a-person issue. As a person who respects the words of the founding fathers, I think we may have some

traction to go back to what Jefferson and Madison actually wrote.

MATTHEW: You want to bring back slavery?

MARK: No, no! Of course not. That would be crazy. It's just that the founding fathers wrote, actually wrote, in ink, that Africans should be counted as three fifths of a person. If we restore the original intent, that would have consequences for redistricting, for voting, land owning and everything else. I'm just saying.

JOHN: Matthew, let's don't get out over our skis here. I want you and Mark to take the next two weeks and focus on delivering a working policy document on your abortion idea. That will be hard enough to get Congress to choke down, let alone re-visiting the three-fifths proposition. Let's circle back at the end of next week and see what you have on paper. I'll make some calls and take the temperature, of the Oval and the Capital. I think I'll call Jude over at Justice and float the trial balloon with him. What do you think?

MARK: I'm excited.

MATTHEW: Yeah, we could really make a move.

JOHN: All right, fellas. Let's get moving!

MARK: Yes, sir!

MATTHEW: Yes, sir!

(end)

Tears into Wine

By Rick Regan

September 3, 2020

This is the story of a family when the father becomes ill and they are visited by Aphrodite.

Characters:

OLIVIA, the mother

TONY, the son

AGATHA, Olivia's sister

GINNIE, the human appearance of Aphrodite

Players:

Olivia	JC Marshall
Tony	Ed Backes
Agatha	Lyn Peticolas
Ginnie	Maura Vincent

Scene 1: kitchen/dining room table, in a comfortable American home

(At the table is Olivia, the mother and Tony, high-school aged son)

(OLIVIA reading a newspaper, sipping coffee at the table)

(TONY eating breakfast cereal, with juice, and reading his phone)

(OLIVIA's phone rings)

OLIVIA: (into phone) Zush? Are you there? Zush?

(listens) Are you there now? What did the doctor say?

(listens) What?! What?! Wha... Oh my god.. Just come home. Just come home. I'll be here.

(hangs up)

TONY: Uh, mom? What was that all about?

OLIVIA: Oh Anthony. Your father was at the doctor. They said he is very sick. He's coming home.

TONY: He doesn't seem sick. Was he feeling sick? He doesn't look sick.

OLIVIA: He was getting these headaches at night. They were keeping him up so he wanted to talk to a doctor to see if there is something he could take for it.

TONY: But... they found something else?

OLIVIA: Mmm-hmm. I don't know the details. He'll be home in a little while. But you should go to school. He can fill you in on the details tonight.

TONY: I think I should probably stay here. School can wait.

OLIVIA: Honey, you're a senior. This is your last year, last three months. You are going to graduate soon. You can't be missing classes when you are so close to the end. Go, go.

TONY: But mom...

OLIVIA: Go. Go, I don't want to hear another word.

TONY: OK, but call me if there is an emergency or something.

OLIVIA: I will. You just relax and do good in school today.

TONY: (gets up to leave) Yes, mother... (exits)

OLIVIA: (sits quietly, then fiddles with her phone, after a pause the phone rings)

Agee? Oh, thank heavens. Listen, I just got off the phone with Xander. He was at the doctor's office.

They said he has tumors in his brain. Agee, I'm so scared!

AGATHA: (through phone) Oh my god! Olivia, what are you going to do?

OLIVIA: I don't know. I don't know what to do. I don't have any of the details, about the tumors or about the treatment. About anything. I don't know what to do.

AGATHA: Olivia. Ok. Let's take a moment here. Take a deep breath. Now, let's pray for a minute.

OLIVIA: That's good. Yeah. You do it.

AGATHA: *Dear Jesus, look down on your loyal servant Olivia, and her humble husband Xander, for their love and devotion to you, dear Lord. Keep Olivia and Xander close to your heart as Xander fights whatever dreadful problem he has in his head. Dear Jesus, we trust in your love and see this time as a challenge to our faith but know that whatever happens will be by your plan and your love. In Jesus' name we pray.*

OLIVIA: *Amen.* Thank you, Agatha. I feel better already.

AGATHA: Olly, you let me know what the outlook is and I will come and stay with you for a while.

OLIVIA: You don't have to do that. We'll be alright.

AGATHA: No, Olly. I have seen this before. The time is shorter than you can imagine and more terrible than you can believe. We'll have to do it together. You were there for me when I had my surgery.

OLIVIA: We'll do it together. I will call you later.

AGATHA: OK. Bye sweetie.

OLIVIA: Bye. (disconnects)

Scene 2: Kitchen, at table

AGATHA: (Sitting, reading the paper, sipping coffee)

TONY: (enters, sees Agatha)

Aunt Agatha. You're up. I didn't expect to see you so early.

AGATHA: Your mother wanted to get to the hospital early today. Are you going over?

TONY: Well, there is not really much to see, is there? You've seen him. There is not much left of him.

AGATHA: He is still your father. You should spend as much time as you can with him now.

TONY: Because he won't be around soon? At this point I wish it was all over, you know? I mean, I don't want him to die but it is just so hard on everybody else. It's like our lives are just all on hold until he either gets better or dies. I mean, I'm sorry, but I am just speaking the plain truth.

AGATHA: I know it is hard. It's hard on you. It's hard on your mother. It's hard for everybody. But it is most difficult for your father. Xander is fighting for his life in a hospital bed. And do you know why? It's for you. He wants to see you grow up.

TONY: I am grown up. I'm 18. I just graduated.

AGATHA: I didn't mean that you are not an adult, but that he wants to see you succeed in your life. But he has to fight for his own life first. You should be there to give him the courage to keep fighting. Do you understand what I mean?

TONY: Yeah, I know. But he is so knocked out with the drugs, when he is even awake, he doesn't know what day it is. He doesn't recognize me or anybody.

AGATHA: That's just the drugs talking.

TONY: Whatever.

AGATHA: Are you doing something else today?

TONY: Well, I was going... I am picking... I..., I don't know.

AGATHA: Anthony, just say it. What's going on?

TONY: I was headed to pick up a friend and we're going to go to the lake today.

AGATHA: Ah, I understand. A girl?

TONY: Yeah.

AGATHA: I see. Well perhaps the energy of youth *should* be spent living, not hovering over the dying. You should go, take her to the lake.

TONY: You really think so?

AGATHA: That's why you were heading out early, isn't it? To slip out without being seen. Or getting the third-degree from old Aunt Agatha. No, you go and have some fun. Put this all out of your mind for a while.

TONY: OK. Thanks. I'll see you later. And, please don't tell Mom.

AGATIIA: It's alright. She'll understand. She was young too.

TONY: (exits)

AGATHA: *Dear Jesus. Please keep that boy safe. Give him a nice girl who can love him and fill his heart with kindness and peace. And for Xander, please keep his heart beating and his mind clear, so that he can recover, to love you even more on into the future. And dear Lord, look out for Olivia. Please send her a sign that the world will be alright again. In Jesus' name, we pray. Amen.*

(Knock on the sliding glass door, facing the back yard. Agatha gets up to open the door. A young woman comes in.)

GINNIE: Uh, I'm sorry. Is this the Malloy residence? Is Tony at home?

AGATHA: You are looking for Anthony? He just left.

GINNIE: He said we were going to the lake today.

AGATHA: Ah, you must be the girl.

GINNIE: The girl?

AGATHA: I think he was going to pick you up. Did you miss him?

GINNIE: I tried the front door bell but I didn't hear anything so I came around back. My name is Ginnie.

AGATHA: Hello, Ginnie. Is that short for something?

GINNIE: Well, technically my name is Gloria, but since I was a little kid people called me "G" or Ginnie.

AGATHA: I see. Well why not call Anthony and tell him you are here.

GINNIE: Yeah, I'll text him. (Fiddles with phone) There.

AGATHA: He'll be back soon. Why don't you sit down.

GINNIE: (she sits at the table) Are you Mrs. Malloy, Tony's mom?

AGATHA: No, that's my sister. I'm staying with the family for a while. Anthony's father is quite ill.

GINNIE: I heard. He's in the hospital, right?

AGATHA: Yes. I don't think it will be long now.

GINNIE: That's too bad. I'm so sorry.

OLIVIA: (enters) Hey, Agee. How's it going here? Oh, who are you?

GINNIE: I'm Ginnie.

AGATHA: She's a friend of Anthony's. They are going up to the lake today.

OLIVIA: Hmmm… (sigh)

(Olivia sits down. She puts her head down and takes the hands of Agatha and Ginnie)

I don't know if can take it. I don't know. I don't think he's going to make it. (crying)

GINNIE: Oh, Mrs. M, I am so sorry. Tony has been telling me everything and it is so bad.

AGATHA: Stay strong, Ollie.

OLIVIA: I don't think I can, Ag. I feel like I am going to break into a million little pieces. I wish I could do it for him. I wish I could give myself up, so he could live. But I can't do anything. Nothing.

AGATHA: Olivia, let's say a quick prayer. Can we? Ginnie, do you mind?

GINNIE: No, no… go ahead.

OLIVIA: Yes, let's pray. You do it, Ag.

AGATHA: *Dear lord, almighty God, savior of the world, dear loving Jesus. In this dark time, show us the light. Pour your salvation into our hearts so that we can be strong. Lift us, O Lord, and bring us the peace of knowing your glory. Look upon Xander and fill him with your healing power. We beg of you, as we pray in His name. Amen.*

OLIVIA: *Amen.*

GINNIE: Ah-mun, Ra.

(Ginnie slowly stands, keeping hold of Agatha's & Olivia's hands. She stands tall and looks down at them. Her voice is stronger and more commanding now.)

AGATHA: Amunra?

GINNIE: That was his name, when I knew him. Amun-Ra, great pharaoh of the land of Egypt. He was a god then too. Like me.

OLIVIA: Excuse me?

AGATHA: A god? Like you?

(Agatha and Olivia take their hands back warily)

GINNIE: That was, oh, seven or eight thousand years ago. A different time. And the people, the Egyptians, worshiped him and called out to him. Amun-Ra! Amun-Ra! Sun God. Mightiest. So powerful that we still say his name in our prayers. Ah-mun.

AGATHA: I don't think that's what it means.

GINNIE: It doesn't matter. I have been sent here to help you. My father has heard your prayers. And here I am.

OLIVIA: Who are you?

GINNIE: I am Aphrodite. Ten thousand years old. Goddess of women and wisdom. I am there, holding your hand when you meet your first love. When your baby is coming, I am there. When there is war and despair in the land, I am here for you. With you. I am alive, forever, because I am needed to hear when a girl is crying, or a mother has lost a child. Or a husband. I am with you. I hear your prayers.

AGATHA: But what about Jesus?

GINNIE: Oh, a lovely man. So gentle. So wise. And the women with him, they were the ones who wanted to change the world. I was there with them when... well, you know. So sad.

OLIVIA: Oh, Aphrodite. Beautiful Aphrodite. Why have you come? Is my husband dead? Can you save him?

GINNIE: I wanted to see you first. I wanted to hear your prayer.

OLIVIA: All I can ask for is forgiveness for my sins.

GINNIE: Nonsense. The sins of women, most women anyway, are like rain clouds at night. All is washed away by morning. Do not worry about sin. Be concerned with love.

OLIVIA: But I am! I am concerned with love. I love my husband. I would do anything for him. I would sacrifice myself if I could.

GINNIE: Well, you can. But I am not interested in you sacrificing yourself.

OLIVIA: But I'll do it. Can you save him if I give you my soul?

GINNIE: Your soul is not yours to give away. A god may take it. A god may extinguish it. But mortals cannot give their souls away to a god.

AGATHA: This is nonsense. You are not a god. You are Anthony's girlfriend. I just opened that door a minute ago.

GINNIE: Hmm. So many prayers but so little faith. Taste your coffee now.

AGATHA: (inspects cup) It has changed. It is not coffee anymore. It is ... wine. A sweet golden wine. How did you do that?

OLIVIA: I believe, Aphrodite. I believe. What must I do to save my husband?

GINNIE: Olivia I see into your heart and know that you love your man. And I see that you love Anthony. But do you love me?

OLIVIA: You? Oh! Yes! Yes, I love you very much. Yes, I love you very much.

GINNIE: Yes. And you are willing to make a sacrifice, to me, for the life of your husband?

OLIVIA: Yes! Yes, anything. I will give you whatever you want.

AGATHA: Careful Ollie...

GINNIE: I have become very fond of your son, Anthony.

OLIVIA: Anthony?

GINNIE: He is tall and handsome. He pleases my eye. He is funny and kind. I want to keep him.

AGATHA: What do you mean, keep him?

GINNIE: I will take him to my island, above the sea, and there he can be immortal. He will be with me.

OLIVIA: He will be immortal? Will he be a god too?

GINNIE: No, only gods are born gods. He is a man, but he will be under my protection.

OLIVIA: Forever?

GINNIE: For as long as I want him and he pleases me.

AGATHA: Does Anthony know anything about this? He was trying to slip out unnoticed this morning.

GINNIE: I have told him that he pleases me, and he will save his father if he comes with me.

OLIVIA: Oh god! This is terrible. Why do I have to give up my son?

AGATHA: You said you would give up anything. Will you give up Anthony?

OLIVIA: Oh god! Why do I have to choose? Can't it be something else? I will give myself up.

GINNIE: I want Anthony. Do you want Xander?

AGATHA: Ollie, this can't be happening. This can't be real. There is no Aphrodite. That is just legend.

OLIVIA: But what if she can heal him? What if she can save Xander for me? She turned your coffee into wine. Didn't she? Here, give it to me. I want to taste it.

(Olivia takes the cup and drinks the wine)

AGATHA: Olly!

OLIVIA: Oh, Agee, it is so wonderful! It is so smooth and sweet, and it lifts the chains from my heart. Thank you Aphrodite. I can see clearly now.

GINNIE: Then you will offer Anthony for me?

OLIVIA: Hear me. I will give Anthony to Ginny, not to Aphrodite. If Xander is to die, then he will live on in our son. I will not have him gone away forever. If you want him, as a woman, then I give you *my* blessing. But I cannot trade my son away. I will not. No.

GINNIE: I see. Then you will leave Xander to Fate.

OLIVIA: But Aphrodite. Do not abandon me. Do not leave me alone in the darkness. I need you.

GINNIE: I will not abandon you.

OLIVIA: Now that I know the truth of the gods, that the gods are real, I know that I need you and I will call out for you. Will you abandon me?

GINNIE: I will be by your side. I will not abandon you.

OLIVIA: My husband is about to die, and I will be in the darkness for a long time. I need you. Will you abandon me?

GINNIE: I will not abandon you. I will hold your hand in the darkness. I will light the candles and twinkle the stars. I will not abandon you.

OLIVIA: Oh god, I am so scared! (weeping) I'm going to be all alone!

GINNIE: (takes Olivia's hand) I am with you. We will bear it together.

AGATHA: (takes Ginnie's other hand) We're here for you, Olly.

OLIVIA: (weeping)

(sound of Tony coming in)

TONY: (enters) Ginnie, what are you doing here?

GINNIE: Anthony, I have told them of my offer. Xander is to live and you to come with me, and be an immortal on my island in the sea. But your mother has refused.

TONY: Mom! We can save Dad. Don't you understand?

OLIVIA: I understand. I know I can't lose you. I won't trade your life away.

TONY: Then I will.

AGATHA: What?

TONY: If I go with her, she will heal Dad. I'm going to save him. I'm going with her.

AGATHA: Anthony, this isn't real. She can't heal him. There is no island in the sea.

TONY: Aunt Agatha, you are the one who's always praying. Praying for Jesus to do something, to heal Dad. What if it was Jesus standing here instead of her? Would you believe then?

OLIVIA: Anthony! Don't go! You don't know what it is, how it is going to be.

TONY: I have to, Mom. I have to, to save Dad.

OLIVIA: You don't have to. You can stay here with me.

TONY: I want to go.

OLIVIA: What?

TONY: I want to start my life, Mom. I want to see the world and live a life of adventure, not just stuck here.

OLIVIA: But I love you, Anthony.

TONY: I love you too. But I want to get my life going, and if this will save Dad, then I'm going.

OLIVIA: Aphrodite, where will you take him? Can I come and see him?

GINNIE: We will live at my temple at *Pela Paphos*. You can make offerings at the temple.

OLIVIA: But I want him to come back. I want him here.

GINNIE: He is a man and he has decided for himself.

OLIVIA: I forbid this!

TONY: Mom, I'm an adult now.

OLIVIA: But I am still your mother!

AGATHA: Olivia, if he is going to go, perhaps there is another way.

OLIVIA: What do you mean, another way? I'm not going to give up my son.

AGATHA: Madam goddess, would you send young Anthony home for six months of the year to visit his family, tend to the fields and vines, help his father with the flock? And then he could go back with you in the winter.

OLIVIA: Agatha, how could you?

AGATHA: Olivia, would you send him if you knew he will be coming back? Think on it.

OLIVIA: (to Aphrodite) Do you promise you will send him back in six months?

GINNIE: I could fly him on a cloud.

OLIVIA: And then he could go back with you?

GINNIE: I will miss him while he is here and I will be glad to see him return.

AGATHA: And you will heal Xander? Today?

GINNIE: I think that now depends on you, Agatha.

AGATHA: Me?

GINNIE: You have so many prayers and yet you still do not believe. I have turned your coffee into wine. I have turned her tears to joy in the hope of healing her husband. But I do not know if I have turned your heart. Is it still a stone?

AGATHA: But I have love in my heart. Look around.

GINNIE: But you do not love me, Agatha. You prayed for help. You prayed for divine signals. You prayed for a miracle. And here I am. I am Aphrodite and I am standing right in front of you. Do you still not believe? Do you not love me?

AGATHA: Madam goddess, I am confused. I am a simple woman. I do not claim to know the way of God's plan. For me, or anybody.

GINNIE: But you call on God for aid. You summoned me! Do you still not believe in the power above and all around you?

AGATHA: But... Aphrodite, I don't know. I don't know anything.

GINNIE: Well, yes. I suppose I asked too much for you to understand the power of your own incantations and appeals to heaven. You are a mortal. I have seen in ten thousand years every kind of ignorance, poverty, suffering and anguish. I stand beside to help. To hold even your hand. Agatha, look. See. I am real. I am here. I am Aphrodite.

AGATHA: But the wine. How did you do that?

GINNIE: That was just a small favor. Here is the miracle.

AGATHA: Miracle?

(Olivia's phone rings in her purse. She fishes it out and answers.)

OLIVIA: Oh, my god! Xander? Is that you? Is that really you?

GINNIE: (to Tony) Now we go.

(Tony and Ginny exit through the sliding glass door out to the back yard)

AGATHA: (seeing them leave) Wait! Anthony...

OLIVIA: (into phone) Xander, it is so great to hear your voice. How are you feeling?

(she listens) Today? OK, I'm coming right over. I love you, darling. I will be there in soon.

(Hangs up phone)

AGATHA: What's going on? Is he all right?

OLIVIA: They said the tumors are gone. They say he can come home, today!

AGATHA: That's wonderful! I can't believe it.

OLIVIA: Neither can I. But I have to go. Thank you, Agee. Goodbye!

AGATHA: God speed!

(Agatha looks around, then sits. She picks up the coffee cup.
)

Gasp! It's full again! With the wine!

(She sips from the cup)

(end)

Swinging with Swingers!

By Rick Regan, September 30, 2020

This is the story of a cross-country bicycle traveler who gets arrested after getting in a fight with some *swingers* in a rural, mountain town in north Georgia. The local sheriff likes to keep his town safe, so he arranges a ride for him out of town.

Characters:

SHERIFF	Local Sheriff
RAY	traveler
DRIVER	truck driver in the diner
Waitress	diner waitress

Players:

Sheriff	JC Marshall
Ray	Lyn Peticolas
Driver	Celia Gannon

Note:

This was presented with the genders inverted, so the male characters all became female characters, and the players were female.

Scene 1: Coffee shop in truck stop, middle of the night, very rural north Georgia

    (Ray is handcuffed behind his back.)

    (POLICE brings RAY into a coffeeshop, inside a truckstop.)

SHERIFF: Look here boy, I was having a real quiet night until I got the call about you. Sit down there.

    (indicates a booth, Ray sits)

    (Sheriff turns to a man seated across the aisle in another booth, where a middle-aged black man in a cap sits reading, or more specifically trying to avoid seeing and hearing the officer.)

    You the driver of that rig with the Tennessee plates?

DRIVER: Yes, sir.

SHERIFF: Now listen here. Don't you go nowhere 'till I tell you.

DRIVER: Yes, sir.

    (Sheriff sits in the booth across from Ray. A familiar waitress brings two cups of coffee, one with a straw for Ray.)

SHERIFF: What's your name?

RAY: Ray.

SHERIFF: Ray what?

RAY: Just Ray.

SHERIFF: (sneering) Don't fuck with me, boy.

RAY: Sir.

SHERIFF: So, Just-Ray, what is going on? The short version. I don't have all night.

RAY: Well, so this guy, Jack, challenged me to a drinking contest.

SHERIFF: Uh huh. Then what?

RAY: He lost. So...

SHERIFF: You banged his wife.

RAY: I was banging the guy's wife, and he got mad about it.

SHERIFF: You were banging Dawn?

RAY: Yeah. You know Dawn?

SHERIFF: (laughs) Serves Jack right, the old snake.

RAY: So you know Jack?

SHERIFF: And Dawn. Banged her myself a few times, but not in a while.

    It is never a slow night when Jack and Dawn are here. Let me get this straight, Jack challenged you to a drinking contest. And then what?

RAY: So that was the bet. He lost. Passed out. Then when he woke up, he attacked me.

SHERIFF: It didn't look like he attacked you. It looked like the scene of a man who discovers another man raping his wife, and when he goes to defend the good woman, the rapist attacks the brave husband. That's what it looked like. As well as causing a disturbance in a boarding house.

RAY: Wait? Rape? What?! She wanted me to. She was all for it.

SHERIFF: Yeah? You can tell the jury. I'm sure they will believe you, Just-Ray.

RAY: Wait, no. The landlady will tell you that's not what happened. She brought up the beers for me.

SHERIFF: She's the one who called in about the disturbance.

RAY: What?

SHERIFF: Just for clarity, so I have it right for the judge, you attacked the man first, then ordered beer to drink while you raped his wife? You are a monster. That jury is going to throw you in a hole.

RAY: Look, this is all wrong. It is nothing like that. She was into the it. I'm not, like, some rapist.

SHERIFF: Is that right?

RAY: I am just a guest at the hotel. I am on a cross-country trip. My bike is there. My ID, my wallet.

SHERIFF: Cross country trip?

RAY: Yeah. I rode here on my bicycle.

SHERIFF: Where you headed?

RAY: Trying to make it to Chattanooga, if I can get out of this town.

SHERIFF: Look here, Jack and Dawn come up here from Atlanta every couple of months. They stir up trouble every damned time. Flo at the B&B calls me ahead and I block out the schedule and wait for it. This is my county and I keep a lid on that kind of shit. But Jack is good for business. Real regular customers and pay top-dollar. So, yours-truly sweeps up the bullshit, and they go back to Atlanta.

RAY: Look, man. I get it. You are the lawman and keep things under control. I just want to get some sleep and ride out of here on my bicycle before the sun comes up.

SHERIFF: Oh, we're going to do better than that.

RAY: What do you mean?

(The Sheriff stands up and walks over to the table across from Ray.)

SHERIFF: Hey, driver.

DRIVER: (straight ahead, not look at the Sheriff.) Can I help you, officer?

SHERIFF: Where you headed, driver?

DRIVER: Memphis, sir. Got a load from Knoxville.

SHERIFF: Is that right? What kind of load would that be, that you are hauling from Knoxville to Memphis?

DRIVER: Yes sir. Dishwashers. Picked them up at the Frigidaire plant. Knoxville.

SHERIFF: Now if I was to inspect that load of dishwashers, I would just find dishwashers. Is that right?

DRIVER: Yes sir. Far as I know. Maybe they put in washing machines? I don't know.

SHERIFF: So you don't really know what you are carrying?

DRIVER: Far as I know, it's dishwashers, sir.

SHERIFF: There wouldn't be any moonshine in that load, now would there?

DRIVER: Moonshine? Oh, no sir.

SHERIFF: You come out of Knoxville, headed to Memphis and you come all the way down here to north Georgia? Seems a long way, out of the way. Don't you think?

DRIVER: I follow the route they give me, sir.

SHERIFF: Oh, they tell you to come all the way down here, instead of going to Memphis directly with those dishwashers? Don't those folks in Memphis need those dishwashers? Don't they have dishes just piling right up? While you are down here in Clayton, Georgia drinking coffee? That doesn't seem right, now does it?

DRIVER: I go where they tell me. I just drive the truck, sir.

SHERIFF: You just go where they tell you? Uh-huh. And they didn't tell you to swing down to Clayton to swap a few barrels of moonshine for a few bales of marijuana, did they? Across state lines.

DRIVER: No sir

SHERIFF: And if I went out into the back of that truck, I wouldn't find that whiskey or that weed, would I?

DRIVER: No sir.

SHERIFF: Now don't you lie to me, boy. Here's what we're gonna do. We're going to decide. We're going to make a choice, right here.

DRIVER: What's that?

SHERIFF: Now you and I could go out to that truck and look at them dishwashers.

DRIVER: Sir?

SHERIFF: And if I find that you have been lying to me, you are going back to jail. You been to jail, ain't ya?

DRIVER: Yes, sir. Don't want to go back, sir.

SHERIFF: I understand. Oh yeah.

              Or, you can head on out of here. And you can take my friend here with you up to Chattanooga. He's on a trip and he needs a ride. I thought, as a favor, you might carry my friend up there to Tennessee. You understand, boy?

DRIVER: I understand. Take that man to Chattanooga.

SHERIFF: That's right. That's a good choice. And, I would recommend that y'all two get going. Like now.

     (Driver looks down at a half a plate of beans and eggs in front of him. He moves to get up.)

SHERIFF: One more thing, driver. Be sure to tip the waitress. They work awful hard. I think five-hundred dollars would be about right.

DRIVER: (shaken) I don't know if I can..

SHERIFF: Or maybe you want to change your choice and we go look in that truck? Makes no never-mind to me. I am fine with whatever your choice is. I was just hoping that you could help my friend get on up to Chattanooga is all.

DRIVER: My folding money is up in the truck. If you'll allow me, I'll be sure to leave the right money, sir.

SHERIFF: Well get on then.

     (Driver exits. Officer waves to Ray, takes off the handcuffs.)

SHERIFF: Now, Just-Ray, I don't want to hear about you again. I don't want to see you around here again. You hear?

RAY: But my bike and my stuff. It's all still back at the hotel.

SHERIFF: I don't give a damn. You are going to leave right now and not stop until you are out of the state of Georgia. That clear enough for you?

RAY: Yes sir.

(Driver returns and puts five one-hundred-dollar bills on the table.)

(Sheriff gently picks up the money.)

SHERIFF: I will make sure these get into the proper hands. I wouldn't want somebody else to make off with your generous tip.

(Ray and Driver exits)

(Officer slip one of the bills to the waitress.)

(Scene 2)

    (Outside, Ray and Driver get in unmarked box truck.)

    (The driver revs the engine and puts the truck in gear. They lurch forward and head down the highway in the dark.)

    (inside the truck, down the highway a few miles)

RAY: OK. Pull over.

DRIVER: What?

RAY: Pull over. I've got to go back and get my bike and my stuff.

DRIVER: The hell I will. No, I'm not stopping until we are well clear of this place. We're way up here in the woods and I am not stopping for nobody.

RAY: But I have to go back and get my bike.

DRIVER: Get a new bike. Or an old bike. But forget that bike. It's gone.

RAY: What?

DRIVER: We are getting the hell out of here and I'm glad for it. I don't like this business one bit. If we get caught they going to throw me back in the joint and I'm never going to get out. They going to throw you in too. Accessory.

RAY: Accessory? Accessory to what?

DRIVER: Man, are you a fool? That cracker knew I got a full load of weed back there? Why do you think I come through this goddamn town? There ain't nothing here but bootleggers and pot growers. Who do you think comes up here?

RAY: I don't know what you are talking about man. Just stop the truck. I'll walk back.

DRIVER: Hell no you won't. He will be coming up this highway behind me, just to make sure we're gone. If he finds you walking back, he will pick you up and then chase me down.

    He'll probably shoot me in the back of the head and throw me down into these woods. Then, he'll sell all the weed back to the dudes that done grown it. They'll sell it again, no problem. Get another nigger drive the truck.

RAY: Come on man. I got to get my stuff.

DRIVER: No. Forget it. They got bikes in Chattanooga.

RAY: But I've got nothing. No ID. No phone. No money.

DRIVER: Here.

(Driver reaches up to the visor. He pulls down a wallet. In the open wallet, there is probably ten thousand dollars in cash. He pulls out a fifty and passes it to Ray.)

DRIVER: That will get you a little ways.

RAY: So you had the money back there at the restaurant?

DRIVER: Oh I got the money. I had the money with me. I wouldn't leave all this out here in the truck.

RAY: So what did you go out to the truck for?

DRIVER: To hide my gun. I had to decide whether I would shoot that sumbitch cracker or just pay him the bribe and move on. I was all decided I was going to get rid of that trash, but when I got to my truck and looked at that gun, I thought, well, five hundred dollars was probably just like a tax, so I hid the gun. And everybody has to pay tax. Even me. Even if it ain't legal, still got to pay the tax. So I paid it and we're out of there.

RAY: Where's the gun?

DRIVER: Where I need it. Anyhow I didn't figure on carrying you up here. But if that is what it takes to get clear out, I carry you.

RAY: Thanks man.

DRIVER: And when we get there, just go on. And don't tell nobody nothing.

[end]

Tina Leary, Psychic

By Rick Regan

October 2020

This is a story of a woman who moves back to her small hometown to look after her ailing mother. To fill her time, she opens a psychic reading salon.

Characters:

GAIL	realtor
PHOEBE	recent college graduate
TINA	professional psychic
ROD	lovesick young man
DEAN,	middle-aged man
CHRISTOPHE	spy master
JANICE	high-school friend

<u>Players:</u>

Gail	Lyn Peticolas
Phoebe	JC Marshall
Tina	Maura Vincent
Rod	Rick Regan
Dean	Ed Backes
Christophe	Chris Gannon
Janice	Celia Gannon

Scene 1: empty office space, for rent.

(Probably an old house, converted to a comfortable suite for business, small town in western Maryland)

(GAIL is a realtor, showing the office space for rent)

GAIL: Here you go. Ready to move in. Great location. I think it is perfect for you.

TINA: This is nice. It is just as you described it. I'll take it.

GAIL: Wonderful. I have your deposit. So here you go. Here are the keys. Congratulations!

(GAIL hands TINA the keys)

TINA: I already have a sign made. "Tina Leary, Psychic", plus the website for making appointments. I used to have a phone number on it, but nobody wants to call anymore.

GAIL: Tell me about it. You cannot get anybody on the phone anymore, let alone meet in person.

TINA: Well, I really appreciate your help with this. I will get a rug and some furniture in here and get started.

GAIL: What brings you up to our little town, if I might ask?

TINA: My mother. She has been declining for the last few years. I've been coming up from DC every so often to see her, watch her progress.

GAIL: Is she still on her own?

TINA: Well that's the thing. It is time to move her into a long-term care place. She really cannot look out for herself anymore. That's why I came up, to help her make the move. But it is a slow process and I thought I might as well fill my days constructively, instead of the two of us staring at each other all day.

GAIL: Is she from here? Would I know her?

TINA: You probably saw her working at my father's pharmacy here in town when I was growing up. Dad ran Leary Family Pharmacy for many years.

GAIL: Oh yes, of course. Leary's, right. I remember your father. He was a sweet man.

TINA: Yes, thank you. He and mom really enjoyed having that place, meeting all the people. You get to know the whole town when you run the pharmacy.

GAIL: Gosh, yes, I suppose.

TINA: But now Mom is on her own and I came up to help with the move.

GAIL: So, psychic, eh?

TINA: Yeah. Psychic.

GAIL: Huh.

TINA: You... want a quick reading?

GAIL: Would you?

TINA: Sure. Give me your hand.

(GAIL gives TINA her hand for a palm reading. TINA rubs it and then looks at it.)

TINA: Let's see. Hmm... Married, 2 kids, realtor for seven years, worried about your older daughter and fully trust your husband.

GAIL: Wow! That's amazing! You could see all that in my hand?

TINA: No. That was on your Facebook profile that I checked before I came over today.

GAIL: Oh. So... You don't have ESP?

TINA: Oh, I'm psychic alright. Look, here's what you really want to know – you are thinking about having an affair with someone close to you. I wouldn't recommend it. The chaos and the pain of the breakup will leave lasting scars – on everyone. That said, your dissatisfaction with your husband is normal. Talk to him and it can get better.

GAIL: (shivers) Oh my! You saw all of that?

TINA: Yes. Listen, you are a good person. Don't worry about it.

GAIL: Amazing.

TINA: Yeah, I am as amazed as you are. I can't help it. Now then, what are the next steps for the lease?

GAIL: I will get the papers finalized today and bring them by in the morning. You can put your sign up right away.

TINA: Wonderful. OK then. I will see you tomorrow.

GAIL: OK. And thanks for that.

TINA: This is going to be swell.

(GAIL exits)

Scene 2: office, now furnished, morning

    (Note: a large old-fashioned radio stands in the back.)

    (Tina is on her phone, listening to a call)

TINA: Uh-huh. Yeah. It's OK. I'll be back and make us some lunch in a little while... Right. You'll be OK.... Just see what the people on TV are doing and I'll be there soon enough for lunch. OK? I have to go. I'll be there soon. OK. Bye.

    (she hangs up, she looks at the radio)

    (Knock at the door, door opens, Phoebe comes in)

PHOEBE: Hello?

TINA: Come in. You are right on time.

PHOEBE: Oh my god. I've never done this before.

TINA: I bet you say that to all your psychics.

PHOEBE: Oh, no! Am I doing it wrong? Am I messing up?

TINA: No, no, honey. You are fine. Please sit down.

PHOEBE: OK.

    (Both sit)

TINA: Alright. Good. So, relax. You are doing fine. Your name is Phoebe? Right?

PHOEBE: Mm-Hm. Phoebe Brown.

TINA: Well, miss Phoebe Brown, what can I help you with today?

PHOEBE: I don't know. It just seems like, you know, everything is, like, messed up.

TINA: O-kay. Messed up.

PHOEBE: Yeah, and, I don't know. I thought maybe, like, maybe you could, like, see the future or something.

TINA: Sometimes. Sometimes I can do that. Is there anything specific you are thinking about?

PHOEBE: Well, OK, so like, I have a job. I work at the hospital, in the eye clinic? Taking appointments? And, it's, like, boring. Really boring. And I thought after I graduated that, you know, that life would start. And now, it's been a year, and it feels like I am just standing still. Nothing is happening! I want it to go! To start! You know? Like, what am I doing?

TINA: Oh, I see.

PHOEBE: Right! So, like, I don't know. Can you see, like, in the future? Does life start? Do things happen?

TINA: Honey, things always happen.

PHOEBE: Not to me. I have been single for the last three years. All I ever meet is old people at the clinic. I write my own songs and put them on YouTube, but people say I am awful, with no talent, and ugly.

TINA: People can be so terrible to each other. I'm sorry they were mean to you.

PHOEBE: I just feel so hopeless. I want the world to start. I keep waiting for my prince charming to come along but it's been so long. I hoped maybe you could help.

TINA: Right.

PHOEBE: But this is silly. I don't know why I am telling you all of this.

TINA: It sounds like you are struggling. It sounds like you want things to change. And they will. For the better.

PHOEBE: You can see that?

TINA: Well, I'll tell you what, let's do a little exercise.

PHOEBE: OK.

TINA: Now, close your eyes. Quiet your mind. Breathe in. Breathe out. That's it. Now, quiet the mind.

PHOEBE: Hmmm...

TINA: I'm going to put my hands on your head. Just relax. And breathe. You are doing really good.

(TINA puts her hands on the sides of PHOEBE's head. After a moment, TINA sits back down)

PHOEBE: Hmmm...

TINA: OK. That's good. Open your eyes now.

PHOEBE: Did you see anything?

TINA: I see you will live a long and interesting life. You will fall in love, quite soon. And later, there will be family. Interesting holidays and lots of love. But the person near you is very shy and will not initiate contact, make the first move. He is terrified of exposing his feelings. But he loves you.

PHOEBE: Who?! Who is it?

TINA: I don't know. You haven't met him yet. But I can see that you must make the first move. You will have to be the brave one and tell him your feelings first, or else he is gone and the relationship goes away.

PHOEBE: Why do I have to do it? Boys are supposed to go first.

TINA: It is the only way. Otherwise nothing happens.

PHOEBE: But it's not fair.

TINA: Why?

PHOEBE: Because what if I pick the wrong one? He'll think I'm a big dummy.

TINA: You will know in your heart. But think about it. If you reach out, make the first move, your life will change. You will start it up, yourself.

PHOEBE: It sounds impossible.

TINA: It's not. Now, that's the end of our time. Come back next week and let me know how it goes.

PHOEBE: Thank you, doctor.

TINA: Come by any time.

(Phoebe exits)

Scene 3: office, afternoon Note: large old-fashioned radio stands at the back.

TINA: (napping on sofa)

(Knock at the door. ROD comes in)

ROD: I don't know if you take walk-ins. Are you busy?

TINA: Not usually, but you have caught me napping. How can I help you?

ROD: I saw your sign. I've never done anything like this before but, I don't know, maybe it's crazy. But I wondered if you can help.

TINA: I can try. What's troubling you?

ROD: I am hoping... Oh this is stupid. I'm sorry. I shouldn't bother you.

TINA: Nonsense. Come on. Out with it.

ROD: Well, I wondered if you could help me find a girl.

TINA: Just any girl?

ROD: No, no. It's just, like, you see a girl sometimes and it's, like, a lightning bolt. You ever have that?

TINA: Oh yes. Lots of people have that. Cupid has a bow and arrow for a reason, you know, because one minute you are just going along, and then THUNK! You are in love.

ROD: Yes! That's it! So, you can help me? Can you, like, do some psychic stuff?

TINA: It doesn't quite work like that.

ROD : Oh. Yeah. I guess this was silly. I'm sorry.

TINA: No. Wait. Let me look.

(closes her eyes, puts her hands on his head)

Ah, I am getting some energy, but it is all fuzzy.

(opens her eyes, takes her hands off him)

ROD: Yeah. This is dumb. I'm a jerk.

TINA: No, no. Hang on. Here's the thing, keep your eyes open for a couple of days, and if you see her, just go up to her and say "Hello!". Then come back and tell me how it goes.

ROD: Yeah. OK. Sorry. How much do I owe you?

TINA: This one's on the house. But if you want to come back some time and talk about your boss, just make an appointment online and we'll sit down for a talk.

ROD: (wide eyed) Wow! OK. Uh… yeah. Well, OK.

TINA: Anytime.

ROD: But I'm right though, right?

TINA: About your boss?

ROD: That it's a con-game, insurance. I work in an insurance office.

TINA: What do you mean?

ROD: My boss works hard, really hustles, and he wants me to get out there and "eat what you kill", he says, meaning sell a bunch of insurance. But he'll write a policy for someone who can't afford it, or way over cover something, like a boat, say, and they end up paying through the nose. I can't face myself if I'm screwing the customers. I want to call him on it, but people love the guy.

TINA: I can see that you have a bright future in front of you. But you could get stuck in a job if you don't like it. Is there something you would rather be doing?

ROD: Sure! Making movies. Who doesn't want to make movies?

TINA: I don't want to make movies. What kind of movies do you want to make?

ROD: I have an idea of making a documentary about following a charity for a year, showing all the aspects of the operation. The staff meetings, the budgeting, the fundraisers, the donor requests, the actual charity work. That kind of thing. Maybe have a series where we choose a different one each year. Most people don't have any idea how charities really work. Like the breast cancer guys. People think it's all just organizing those walks but that's just a tiny slice of what goes on. I'd like to show that.

TINA: That sounds like a wonderful idea. Is something holding you back from starting?

ROD: Sure, money!

TINA: Maybe your first one could be about getting your production company started. Nobody knows how that all works, how movies get made.

ROD: That's an interesting take on it. I'll kick it around.

TINA: There is a way to get started but you have to do it. But then, you get to do it.

ROD: OK, so, thanks for this.

TINA: Glad to help. Stop in and let me know how it goes. (They shake hands and he exits)

Scene 4:   office, early afternoon.

Note: large old-fashioned radio has moved to the opposite side of the room

(Tina is on the phone)

TINA: (into the phone) I know, Mother. You'll have to get used to it. It's going to be a little different now.... Uh-huh.... Uh-huh... Well, listen, I will come and visit you when I am finished up here. OK. Alright. Bye.

(Tina hangs up the phone. She looks over at the radio.)

(DEAN enters)

DEAN: Hi. I'm here for my one o'clock.

TINA: Oh, yes. Very good. Come in. Sit here.

DEAN: (sits) Yeah. Uh-huh.

TINA: (Feels a very disturbing, dark energy) So, Mr. Ratcliff, what can I help you with today?

DEAN: Call me Dean. So, you're, like, a psychic?

TINA: That's right. How can I help you?

DEAN: For real?

TINA: Yep.

DEAN: OK then. Can you predict the lottery?

TINA: No. I'm sorry. It doesn't generally work that way. Usually I see human things.

DEAN: OK. OK. So, basketball? NBA?

TINA: Only if you are playing.

DEAN: What about betting?

TINA: You mean, could I tell you if you would lose with one bet and win with another?

DEAN: Right.

TINA: It is not commonly done, but we can try.

DEAN: Really?

TINA: Why not?

(she sees herself being held captive, his Golden Goose. She is worried.)

DEAN: OK, so let me think of a bet. (closes eyes)

TINA: Hmm. Let me see. No, that seems like an unhappy future. But I am not sure if it is the bet. I think, well, the betting itself is making you unhappy.

DEAN: Wait, OK, hold on. Let me try it another way. Try now (closes eyes again)

TINA: Well I see you happy and celebrating but I think you might just be feeling the emotions, not winning the bet.

DEAN: So, you liked that one, huh? Lakers cover the spread on Friday night.

(he makes a note in a small book)

OK.   Try this one. (closes eyes again)

TINA: I see... money, and ... pistols... and some other men. Some women. Is this a hotel? Or an apartment? I'm sorry, I don't see anything about the bet. Just gamblers and gangsters.

DEAN: (angry!) Gamblers and gangsters, huh? Look here, I don't need some broad calling my friends gangsters. I'm connected, you know!

TINA: Then why did you come here, to me today?

DEAN: To see if you could pump the juice for us. You'd get a share. Sure. You want to be here, sweating in this lousy box for the next ten? Reading the tea-leaves for old ladies? Huh? I could make you some dough. Some real bread, you know?

TINA: Yes, I know what you mean.

DEAN: But honey, you got to focus. Get your head in the game.

TINA: I'm not interested in your scheme. Every psychic or seer gets an idea at some point, me too, to parley their skills. But it all comes to dust. Like I said, for me too.

DEAN: You tried to work the angles?

TINA: Horses. Saratoga. It was the Eighties.

DEAN: What happened, you lose?

TINA: No. I won. And won. And won!

DEAN: Hey, now you're talking!

TINA: And then I lost. And lost. And lost.

DEAN: Oh.

TINA: I don't know anything about horses. I got a hot hand and then it went cold. I would have done better if I just flipped a coin.

DEAN: So you stay out of the racket, eh?

TINA: Well, you know, I got a different racket.

    (indicates the office)

DEAN:	Diff... Oh, hey! Ha! Yeah, I got ya.
TINA:	But it is real.
DEAN:	Yeah? So, OK. What do you see with me?
TINA:	Mister Ratcliff, I sense a great dark energy with you. Sinister. A tremendous chaos and confusion surrounding you. You run a business of some sort, but 'money' is blaring like a trumpet. I can't tell why.
DEAN:	So do they whack me? Like Tony?
TINA:	Tony? From the Sopranos?
DEAN:	Yeah. Does somebody put a bullet in the back of my head?
TINA:	I sense a long life, or at least not a sudden end soon. But I do sense a great fear around women. Screaming? I don't know. Should I be afraid, Dean?
DEAN:	Naw. No. I wouldn't hurt a nice lady like you. But I know some working girls, and they can be... dramatic. Everything is an emergency with them. All drama, all the time. I might have to modify their behavior occasionally with some strong words.
TINA:	And the beatings? And the forced sex?
DEAN:	You can see all that?
TINA:	I don't have to. You told me yourself.
DEAN:	OK, look, what are we doing here?
TINA:	I see two pathways for you, Dean. The first one is the path you are on, a short and unhappy path. The other is happy, satisfied and safe, but it is a journey of discovery.
DEAN:	Oh, great. Now I have to go "find myself", or some dippy shit?
TINA:	Not you, Dean. You don't have to find yourself. You must open your eyes to the rest of the world. You have a journey of discovery of the world around you. The people, the animals, the plants, the energy all around you.
DEAN:	Look, lady, this is bullshit.
TINA:	Dean...
DEAN:	I came here and I took up your time. In my world, time is money, so here is payment for the session, even though you couldn't help. Don't let anybody say I stiffed you!

    (Throws cash on the table)

TINA: Alright.

DEAN: I'm out of here. (moves to exit)

TINA: Mister Ratcliff, just one more thing. Thank you for coming here today. And if you want to come back and talk more about some of these things, or anything, please do stop in.

DEAN: Yeah, OK. Sure. (exits)

Scene 5: office.

(Phoebe is already there in a session. Big Radio is still there.)

TINA: OK. Go on. You left work…

PHOEBE: And I think this man is following me. I came to see you so you could see if he is going to kill me.

TINA: (alarmed) Kill you?

PHOEBE: Well, like, lock me in a basement, like that girl in Cleveland. I don't know but she, like, she lived in a locked basement, and he just used her as a sex slave, for years. Is that what's going to happen to me? Am I going to be chained up, like a wild animal, and have, like, sex, on-demand? Do I escape?

TINA: Whoa, whoa, whoa! Slow down. Those kinds of situations are vanishingly rare. That is not likely to happen to you at all.

PHOEBE: Would you look? Pleeeeeaaaaaaassse?

TINA: OK. Hmm… Hmmm… Hmmm…

PHOEBE: What?! What is it? Am I chained up in a dungeon?

TINA: Well, some ropes. You are tied up.

PHOEBE: Oh, no!

TINA: But you are smiling.

PHOEBE: I'm just pretending to like it, so he doesn't …*slit my throat!*

TINA: Well, you are wearing a ring. So is he. And it looks like a bedroom. Kind of a girly bedroom, with flouncy edging on the covers. Not a dungeon.

PHOEBE: Really?

TINA: It's a house. Not far from here. "Watkins Drive"?

PHOEBE: Wait, what!

TINA: That's the street. You are tied up, naked, in a house, on Watkins Drive, in the bedroom, with a man, who seems to be your husband. And…

PHOEBE: What?!

TINA: There are pictures of children on the dresser.

PHOEBE: No!

TINA: Yes. They seem to be your children, but I am not sure if they are his. Umm, he's somebody you knew in high school.

PHOEBE: Jimmy? I have Jimmy's kids?

TINA: No. But there are several of these 'tie-up' nights. I gather his wife is not into it.

PHOEBE: And what about my husband?

TINA: Not clear. The ring usually links to another energy, or person. His does. To, Dolores?

PHOEBE: Dolores? Dolores marries Jimmy?

TINA: But your own ring does not. Is it fake?

PHOEBE: Oh, I wear rings all the time. I don't follow the rules. I'm a rebel like that.

TINA: I see.

PHOEBE: So the guy who is following me, he's not a stalker?

TINA: Hold on. (closes eyes) Hmm... wait! He's looking for you. He's in love with you. Cupid? Oh, yes, I know him. He came here, looking for you. Love at first sight.

PHOEBE: What?

TINA: Well, how about that. That's nice.

PHOEBE: Wait, so he's in love with me? How do I find him?

TINA: Oh, he'll find you. Yes, he's following you. But he is very shy. He will never make the first move. Never!

PHOEBE: But...

TINA: Never. So you have to. He's a nice boy. You'll get on great.

PHOEBE: But what do I say?

TINA: I can see this. You walk up to him and say, *Hello, my name is Phoebe. What's your name?* This will be on Tuesday.

PHOEBE: Tuesday? Oh my god! I have to get ready.

TINA: Well, if that's what you want. Or, you could walk up to him and say, *leave me alone! Stop following me!* And he will. You will never see him again.

PHOEBE: But he loves me!

TINA: yes, but it is your choice.

PHOEBE: How can I just walk up to him and tell him my name?

TINA: Practice.

PHOEBE: What?

TINA: Practice. Like this. Say it to me now, *Hello, my name is Phoebe. What's your name?*

PHOEBE: Uh, OK. *Hello, my name is Phoebe. What's your name?*

TINA: Perfect. Remember that and it will serve you well in your life.

PHOEBE: This is strange.

TINA: OK, here we are. You have to go prepare, and I have another client.

PHOEBE: Oh Miss Tina, thank you so much!

TINA: Good luck and come back to tell me how it goes.

PHOEBE: Thank you, thank you, thank you!

Scene 6: office. Radio is still there

TINA: (on the phone) Oh Mom, don't cry. It will be OK. You just had a little spill, that's all. It's not like the *old ladies* who fall and break their hips. You just had a stumble... Uh-huh. Uh-huh. OK. Alright, Mom. Listen, I have to go now. I have an appointment... Mom, mom. Don't cry. I will be home soon. OK. Alright. Bye now. (Hangs up phone)

(TINA goes to the couch and lays down, her arm over her eyes. She rests for a moment, then the door opens.

Janice enters. JANICE is TINA's age. They were classmates in high school.)

JANICE: Tina, is that you? Tina?

TINA: (sits up, gets up, hugs Janice) Janice! I can't believe it. I haven't seen you in forever. How are you?

JANICE: I heard you were in town. I just had to drop in. It's so good to see you. I heard you were down in DC. You look amazing!

TINA: Gee, thanks. It's so great to see you. Life comes along so fast and we lose touch with our friends. So yeah, DC, you know, one thing happens after another. Before I knew it, I was working, had an apartment and life was on its way. How about you? Do you have family here?

JANICE: You mean, did I just stay here after high school? Well, yeah, kind of. I went to Mount Saint Mary's in Emmitsburg. It was nice but after two years I was bored out of my mind.

TINA: So, you came back to Hancock? It's a *really* small town...

JANICE: I like it. I got a job at the grocery store, and I'm still there. I am managing three stores now and working with the corporate guys in Cincinnati. It's my little slice of the American dream. How about you? You ever get married, have kids?

TINA: I was in a long-term relationship, a while ago, but we both just, I don't know, drifted apart. One day we both looked up and said, *who are you? Who is this person I'm living with?* We cared deeply about each other, but the spark was gone. So, I moved into my own place and that's been it for, shoot, almost a decade now.

JANICE: Does that make you sad? That sounds sad.

TINA: No, it's not like that. I like my life. I like the freedom, the flexibility. But the nights can be cold and lonely.

JANICE: Yeah.

TINA: How about you? Family?

JANICE: Oh, gosh yes. I have two. My sister has three and my brother, he moved to Baltimore. He doesn't have any kids but makes boatloads of money. He has this wonderful apartment overlooking the Inner Harbor. It's beautiful.

TINA: I can picture it. Did you get married?

JANICE: Yeah, I married Mike. He was still waiting for me when I came back from Emmitsburg.

TINA: McKay? Mike McKay?

JANICE: Yeah. We were sweethearts in school and it just never went away. He manages the trucking terminal for the big storage warehouse, on Main, just off Seventy.

TINA: Is that what that is? I've been by there a thousand times and never knew what they do there. Just trucks and boxes, all the time.

JANICE: It's twenty-four hour. My son says he wants to drive a truck. He's seventeen. But his dad says, no way. He says he sees truckers every day and somehow, they get poorer and poorer the more they drive. It's a fixed game for truckers now, what with the Mexican drivers and all.

TINA: I didn't know that.

JANICE: It's all he talks about. But, hey, the real reason I came in is to get a reading. Could we do that?

TINA: Umm, sure. OK. Is there something specific you need help with?

JANICE: Well, it's Mike. He's got this friend who is really into gambling and he's trying to get Mike into it, my Mike. He says it is a sure-thing because they have a way to beat the system, he says. I've never seen anybody win with betting other than getting lucky or cheating. I am worried about him getting in bed with the wrong crowd. I can't afford to lose him if he goes to jail because of some crackpot betting scheme.

TINA: Mike's getting involved with gamblers?

JANICE: Yes. And, I guess, I need to know if it is real or just a hustle for these guys. And they will kick Mike under the bus, or cut him out of the action, ... or worse.

TINA: I don't need to do a reading to tell Mike to stay away from those people. They are into some dirty business. I can't really talk about it, but Mike should stay away.

JANICE: What about a reading though?

TINA:

I can do that. Here, sit down. I'm going to put my hands on your face for a moment. Relax. Close your eyes. Breathe. Breathe.

(Puts her hands-on Janice's face)

Hmmm... Hmmm... Hmmmm....

JANICE:

What can you see?

TINA:

(takes her hands back) I can see you and Mike arguing. Probably over this, maybe something else. I can see your daughter and son watching, absorbing the negative energy. I don't see anything specific, but something is coming between you.

JANCIE:

Well there's been a lot of that.

TINA:

I see two paths. One is continuing with conflict. The other is to be flexible with him. I think that if you give him the flexibility he wants, he comes back to you with more love and appreciation.

JANICE:

Hmmm...

TINA:

It is a funny thing. I've seen it before where one person putting their foot down, smashes a relationship, and other times where the flexibility heals relationships. That's what it looks like.

JANICE:

That dog. I bet he wants to fool around on me too. It has to be that tramp that works at the terminal with him. Well he can stuff it.

TINA:

No, no. I don't see that. I don't sense another person in his heart. Listen, the other path, the one you are on, with confrontation and arguing, it can be very destructive.

JANICE:

He's just jealous because I am the district manager now and he's still dispatching trucks. I make twice as much as him and he wants to be the boss. I'll show him who's the boss. He's going to get a taste of my size-nine up his backside.

TINA:

Janice don't be like that. He loves you. He loves your kids. Don't throw that all away.

JANICE:

Gail, thank you. You see right through his b/s. And I'm going to let him have it when he gets home. Right now, I am so mad I could spit nails. If he wants to play *Ocean's Eleven* like he's some kind of casino kingpin, he's going to fall on his face. It's not like everybody in town doesn't already know what's going on. Bad news travels fast in a small town. That sorry sack of soup...

TINA:

Maybe there are some other things going on, other issues?

JANICE:

Oh, there are other issues. Lots of them. I don't need to get into it, but let's just say there is a reason he was waiting for me here after two years. I was the best opportunity he ever had. He'd still be pumping gas if it wasn't for me getting him that job at the terminal. Hey, I'm sorry. I don't mean to dump all of this on you. That's all I'll say.

TINA: You've been together a long time.

JANICE: Well, maybe not much longer. I'll see myself out. Thank you, Gail. Nice to catch up with you.

(Janice exits)

Scene 7: office

(Gail is already in session.)

(Note: Big Radio has a dust covering over it.)

GAIL: I like what you have done with the place.

TINA: Thanks.

GAIL: And how is your mother doing?

TINA: I had Mom moved over to Calvert House, you know, up the hill. They are taking care of her there.

GAIL: Oh, yes. That's a nice place. My aunt Joy went there. Is she doing well there?

TINA: I don't think so. The move has her very disoriented and the staff called this morning to say that she was not eating. I'm worrying about her.

GAIL: Oh, I'm sorry. This really is the hard part, you know.

TINA: Yeah. I know.

GAIL: So how is business for you?

TINA: Building up traffic. Slow start but I'm happy with it. How did it go with your husband?

GAIL: Well, this is where I need some help. He suspects that I am cheating on him, which I'm not, you know that. But I get the feeling that he may have a little hot something on the side. I think he's cheating on me!

TINA: Oh, that's not good. What do you want to do about it?

GAIL: I want you to tell me if he's running around on me. And put a *hex* on him.

TINA: I'm not sure that I can but I can take a look. We'll see about a hex.

(Tina puts her hands-on Gail's face)

GAIL: Go ahead, look.

TINA: Hmmm.... I'm not seeing any real trouble there. The energy looks balanced. The connection between your rings is fine. I don't know. I don't see anything specific about him, but it looks OK.

(She takes her hands back)

GAIL: Do you think he's being so secret that he could hide from you? Like maybe it's online, with somebody far away? Like an old girlfriend?

TINA: Gail, I am not really picking anything like that up. I wonder if your own thoughts of temptation may be affecting your judgement, of your husband. I feel a heaviness in you. Is there something else bothering you?

GAIL: Hmm... Well... I guess my daughter, Phoebe. She started seeing this guy and now she is going all over town. She stays at his place sometimes. I suppose they are probably having sex. She is just going a hundred miles an hour, is all.

TINA: Hmm... Yes. But she's how old? 22 or 23? She has got to have her own life.

GAIL: She wants her own life, but she is so silly she doesn't know what she's doing. She's never had any common sense. A couple of weeks ago we watched a movie on TV, you know the made-for-TV things on about reality-crime. It was about a woman who was kept as a prisoner after she was kidnapped as a teen. Horrible show. We shouldn't have even been watching it. But I wanted her to see it, to get some understanding about how dangerous men can be.

TINA: I see. How did that go?

GAIL: A flop. Phoebe spent the next two weeks talking about how she was being followed and the man was going to make her a sex slave in a basement.

TINA: I guess it made quite an impression.

GAIL: Well that's her though. She can barely tell what's real and what is some show on TV.

TINA: But the new boyfriend, he's nice, right?

GAIL: (exasperated) She won't bring him over. We've never met him. She says, he's shy. Shy! Hmph! So now I'm pulling my hair out because I'm thinking the guy might literally be trying to lock her in a basement. You know what I mean?

TINA: It sounds like she's growing up. Is that difficult for you?

GAIL: Difficult for me? Why, if I wasn't there to get things moving for her, she would mope around in bed all day. If I weren't pushing her, she wouldn't be... She's just lucky I'm here to guide her.

TINA:	But what about her being, you know, separate from you, is that hard?

GAIL:	What do you mean?

TINA:	That she's her own person, not just an extension of you. Sometimes people have trouble with this aspect of being a parent. Sometimes it is the shock of loneliness. Sometimes it is the loss of purpose, for the parent, to not have the child, well... grown adult, needing you to direct them.

GAIL:	Or need me at all. What am I supposed to do now? She's off gallivanting around with Mr. Right and I am stuck behind by myself.

TINA:	You are not alone though. You have your husband. You have been together for a while now. You are a team, a couple.

GAIL:	Or a three-some, if he has some precious Insta-Influencer sending him nudies all day. I want you to put a hex on him. Make his... thing fall off.

TINA:	Gail, that's not going to help anything. You have to talk to him. Tell him what you are thinking.

GAIL:	He'll just lie about it and deny everything.

TINA:	At least you should tell him that you suspect something. Then you have been honest in the situation. If he is lying, you'll probably know, but you will be truthful.

GAIL:	But what if what he wants isn't me? What if I'm the boring old wife, same old in-and-out, hello and good to know ya'? Out with the old, in with the new.

TINA:	What are you talking about? You are afraid that he is bored with you?

GAIL:	Well I'm bored, anyhow. Why not him too? Just reset and refresh, with all those women in the world just scheming for a good man, my good man. He could snap his fingers and a dozen women would be rubbing his face in it.

TINA:	Gail, hang on. You are getting way ahead of yourself. Listen, the first time you came in here, you were thinking about a tryst with another man. What is really driving all of this? Is your relationship so stale that you both just want out?

GAIL:	I just want him to suffer. Some. Kinda. Because men don't get pushed aside and ignored when they hit middle age.

TINA:	You want him to suffer because you feel invisible?

GAIL:	Right.

TINA: But you are a successful businesswoman, with your own realty practice. Nobody ignores you. Is this about Phoebe?

GAIL: It's like water, slipping out of my fingers. It's like, I've got everything under control. Everything is arranged. Life is going good. And then, one day, I wake up and see everything, gradually, just sliding away. Sliding away, from me. And I see myself, like your mother, losing myself, my house, my family, my life. Everything, they say, *oh Mom, it's not like that anymore. You have to learn the new way*. Like these damned new phones. I have to learn the new 'operating system'. For the phone. The TV. My car. I have to log-in to my car to start it, so it knows it's me, as if it is judging me, watching, tracking. The whole damned thing. And now she's gone, off with mister creepy-weirdo or who knows who. And I'm just left on my iceberg to float off into the sea and freeze.

TINA: (long sigh) That's a lot. That's a lot.

GAIL: Yeah, I know. Look can you just give me a quick read and tell me how it is all going to come out?

TINA: I don't have to. I know that…

GAIL: Please? Just do it. Please?

TINA: OK. Ok.

(puts her hands-on Gail's face)

GAIL: (sigh)

TINA: hmmm…. Hmmm… hmmm… ok.

(removes her hands)

GAIL: Well?

TINA: Will it make you feel any better if I tell you that you will be a grandmother?

GAIL: Really!? Phoebe?

TINA: Not right now. Not right away. But I see you with a house full of little kids, running and playing. And you are there, happy. You are the light to these little ones. You share so much love with them.

GAIL: Oh heavens! Oh my. That changes, I mean. Suddenly, you know. It's, It's, oh what am I worrying about? Maybe Terry is having a fling. Phww! So, what! We've got real work ahead.

TINA: Well?

GAIL: I've got to think about this. There is a lot of planning to do that I haven't even considered. This rearranges everything. But in a good way.

TINA:	OK.
GAIL:	Thank you. This helps so much. I'm so glad you are here.
TINA:	Good. Good.
GAIL:	OK, that's enough. I've got to get going. Thank you again.

(Gail gets up to exit)

TINA:	Great. Well, come by anytime.

(Gail exits.)

(Tina looks at the radio again, with the covering on it)

Scene 8: office, The radio is in the back but now the covering is black

(Tina lies on the sofa, maybe asleep.)

(Knock at the door. Christophe enters)

CHRISTOPHE: Hello? Mrs. Leary? May I come in?

TINA: (rising) Oh, hello. Yes. Come in. Can I help you?

CHRISTOPHE: (comes in, looks around. He spots the radio.) Oh.

TINA: Here, sit. Down. How can I help you?

CHRISTOPHE: I think, rather, that I am come to help you. You are Tina Leary?

TINA: Yes. Who are you?

CHRISTOPHE: My name is Christophe Waterstone. Your mother was Martha?

TINA: Yes. How do you know that?

CHRISTOPHE: I have come down from the War College. For the radio.

TINA: Oh?

CHRISTOPHE: Did she ever, as such, tell you about the radio?

TINA: Well, no. And, come again, the War College?

CHRISTOPHE: Yes. The Naval War College, in Rhode Island. We, well, study war. As it were.

TINA: OK and what does that have to do with mother's old radio?

CHRISTOPHE: She has passed now, I understand?

TINA: Yes, on Monday. She stopped eating and just withered away. She just didn't want to live anymore.

CHRISTOPHE: Hmm. How cruel life can be.

TINA: I'm sorry, what is this all about?

CHRISTOPHE: Your mother was, as it were, a delightful, surprising and quite effective woman, as a spy.

TINA: I think you have the wrong Martha Leary.

CHRISTOPHE: No, no. All the pieces fit. The puzzle is complete. The picture is clear now.

TINA: What?

CHRISTOPHE: Your mother, she had, hmmm…, talents, just as you have?

TINA: Yes, she had great ability. I think she found it to be too much trouble though, working in the pharmacy.

She worked in a pharmacy, with my father, the pharmacist, his assistant. And all the people in town would come in, for whatever the doctor gave them. And she could see, she could feel the suffering. The worried parents of a sick child. The young woman, scared out of her mind. The young men who wouldn't look at her when they were getting their things. The old people and the young people. She would tell me about how she could sense the energies, see the bed in the room with the patient. It weighed on her.

CHRISTOPHE: Well she had, as they say, seen her share of life.

TINA: What are you talking about? A spy, you say.

CHRISTOPHE: Well, in brief, your mother, before she was married, worked in and with the intelligence branches of the government for some years. In some ways, as they say, one never leaves. During the Cold War, there were many hot spots around the globe where the battlespace was mystifyingly opaque. We recruited people who had the *remote viewing* skills.

TINA: Should I be taking notes for this?

CHRISTOPHE: I am afraid that is not, officially, permitted.

TINA: Hush-hush?

CHRISTOPHE: Right-O.

TINA: I see.

CHRISTOPHE: Your mother was stationed, auspiciously, under my direction in Rhodesia. She had started, quite humbly, as a bomb assembler, small rockets and torpedoes that could be used in covert missions. Pocket rockets, you see.

TINA: Oh.

CHRISTOPHE: By the time she had come my way, she had shown great promise and interest in the cloak and dagger business. After her service tests, she came to Africa. Angola first, then under me in Rhodesia.

TINA: My mother, the pharmacist's assistant?

CHRISTOPHE: Yes, that was quite good, wasn't it? An excellent cover, pharmacist assistant. Who suspects the pharmacist's assistant? Brilliant! Her idea, of course.

TINA: Are you for real?

CHRISTOPHE: Quite so, I'm afraid.

TINA: What about the radio then?

CHRISTOPHE: The radio is, as you suspected, not a radio. Or rather, not a standard radio. Oh, it looks like an old antique, tube-type radio. For Jack Benny and the like. But it was, at the time, fantastically futuristic.

TINA: I don't think it ever worked. I never have seen it on at all.

CHRISTOPHE: Well, you know, many of the pieces are missing so one couldn't get it going without knowing how it worked and why. You see, we used these around the world as short-wave radio receivers. You know how a fax machine works, with the sound over the telephone?

TINA: Yes, I am familiar with fax machines.

CHRISTOPHE: This device was a receiver for, as it were, a fax "broadcast", over short-wave radio. We would send messages, encoded of course, to the stations around the world.

TINA: But if it is broadcast, couldn't just anyone listen to it?

CHRISTOPHE: Yes, indeed. And this is where your mother comes in. She noticed, when she was training with the British Navy, that the British officers all listened to the BBC world service over the shortwave. They would synchronize every clock on the ship with the top-of-the-hour tone, broadcast around the world, so that all her Majesty's ships were precisely synchronized. Well, Martha thought this was quite ingenious and when it came time to have a system to broadcast our messages, she came up with a system for the time and frequency for every message, based on the BBC tide broadcast.

TINA: How so?

CHRISTOPHE: During the BBC weather forecast, there is a reading of high tide peak and the time. So, *Falmouth, six-point-nine meters, four twenty-one am*. That sort of thing. So, if the key is *Falmouth*, the frequency would be set to six-point-nine and the broadcast was at four twenty am. It was ever so clever.

TINA: And this is one of those devices.

CHRISTOPHE: Precisely. And I have come to collect it for the US Naval War College, to be used for teaching the spy game. She was still one of ours up until the end, you know. I received her final sign off a few weeks ago.

TINA: That can't be true.

CHRISTOPHE: Her file is classified, as you might guess, but I have a few things for you to sign, for the radio. After fifty years, her file will be de-classified, and you may wish to read all about who she really was.

(hands her a folder)

TINA: I know who she was. She was my mother.

CHRISTOPHE: Indeed.

TINA: Is there anything else?

CHRISTOPHE: That's the end of it.

        (Christophe goes to the radio)

Scene 9: Office, empty now.

    (Tina's sign is turned sideways, leaning against the wall)

TINA: (Enters, walks around, looking for anything left)

GAIL: (Enters) Oh, Hi, Tina. I guess you have it all cleared out, huh?

TINA: Yeah, I'm sad to close up shop but I am going back to DC. I still have my apartment there and now that mom is gone, I must get back to my own life.

GAIL: Yeah, I understand. It is a shame you are leaving though. You helped me so much.

TINA: You get it worked out with your husband?

GAIL: It turns out he wasn't running around on me. He was seeing Phoebe. He just didn't tell me about it. He was worried too about her new boyfriend, so he made a couple of "Dad-dates" with her to check in with her. She's doing OK. He says the boy is smart and funny but painfully shy. But he seems to be good for her and she seems to bring out the good things in him. That's all you can ask for, right?

TINA: For now. Later there will be other things, but for now, we can be happy about what is good.

GAIL: Right.

TINA: So here are the keys, by the way. I think everything is in order.

GAIL: That's it then. Ok. Say, are you a, you know, psychic in DC then?

TINA: No. I have a kind of data company, that looks for missing people, people who just vanish. I have a small team of partners, also with *remote viewing* abilities, and we try to find people. Usually for police or government agencies. Sometimes it is a tax cheat on the run, or a bank robber who is missing. We don't get rich but it's a good living. And we get to use our talents for, usually, good outcomes. Some runaways. Some abductions.

GAIL: Sex slaves?

TINA: Them too. Not often though. Usually the mailman finds those, so the cops don't need us.

GAIL: That is so weird.

TINA: A weird world. And thank you, Gail, for all your help with this. I couldn't have done it without you.

GAIL: Just doing my job. Goodbye Tina.

TINA: Goodbye Gail.

(End)

Way of the Iguana

By Rick Regan

October 8, 2020

<u>Characters</u>:

Jose,	Mexican laborer
Luis,	son and helper
Tomas,	Mexican laborer, friend of Jose
Mother,	tamale maker
Pia,	daughter and tamale seller
Marta,	companion of older Luis

<u>Notes</u>:

This is a story of a Mexican family dealing with the challenges of the modern world, and using allegories to make sense of the situation. The *way of the iguana* is to choose laziness and meaninglessness over productive work and contribution to the family. The father and mother try to convey their spirit of industriousness and decency to the son and the daughter. When the son is older he finds himself in trapped in a world of poverty and despair so he must choose whether he will follow the advice of his father or languish in indolence.

<u>Players</u>:

Jose	Ed Backes
Luis	Chris Gannon
Tomas	Rick Regan
Mother	Maura Vincent
Pia	Lyn Peticolas
Marta	JC Marshall
Stage Directions	
	Celia Gannon

Scene 1: Early morning, building site, Jose and Luis are sitting on stacks of mortar and plaster, waiting to start working

LUIS: Father, how are you this morning?

JOSE: Son, I have eaten. You have eaten. Now we work.

LUIS: Yes.

JOSE: But first a smoke.

(Jose lights a cigarette)

LUIS: Can I smoke?

JOSE: No.

(Luis, he is probably 16, watches his father smoke)

LUIS: Father, why do we work here? Why are we not at home?

JOSE: We are at home.

LUIS: You know what I mean. In *Tabasco*.

JOSE: You mean *Paraiso*? With your mother. Yes, I know what you mean.

LUIS: Why, papa?

JOSE: My son, you are thinking too much. Learning too much. Today we have eaten and today we work.

LUIS: Could we not work at home?

JOSE: This is home.

LUIS: Papa…

JOSE: In *Tabasco* we would get paid in *pesos*. For a day's work, it is nothing. The men are all poor. The women are in even more poverty. The boss, he will find the man who will work for the smallest money. It is no good. Here, *el Norte*, we make enough in a week to send home for your sister and your mother. And you and I, we keep enough so we may eat. Then we work.

LUIS: Yes, father. We eat and we work. How long do we work?

JOSE: Luis, do you know what it is to work?

LUIS: Yes, papa. I carry the tile. I carry the grout. I wash the tools. I sweep. I load. Yes, I know what it is to work. Why do you ask me this? Do you think I do not work? I am here, with you, everyday. We work together. Why do you ask me if I know work?

JOSE: Because you only know what you think is work. This is not work.

LUIS: This is not work? Then why does the man give you the dollars?

JOSE: My son, you are a mule. A donkey. Every step the donkey takes he resents, and thinks the world is unfair to him, whether he carries a heavy load or his bags are empty. And he is right, this donkey. No one cares about how the donkey feels, walking with a load. He is there to walk the load. Do you understand?

LUIS: No. I do not understand. Why do call me a donkey?

JOSE: Because I am a donkey. And you are donkey. No one cares if we are happy to lay the tile. They only care that the tile is smooth, straight and flat. You understand?

LUIS: OK. So, we are here to be donkeys? No, I don't understand.

JOSE: We are here for labor. It could be you or me, or another donkey waiting around the corner. They can always get another donkey.

LUIS: Yes.

JOSE: But that is not work.

LUIS: No?

JOSE: Work is the labor of your heart. When I have an idea and I struggle to make the idea real. Make the idea true, that is work.

LUIS: It sounds like the same thing, papa. Work is work.

JOSE: No, Luis. You and me, we labor as donkeys because the boss will pay us more than we would make in *Tabasco*. But my work is to send money back home. My work is to help you learn and grow, to teach you how to make your own way in the world. My work is what is in my heart. You are in my heart, my son.

LUIS: *Si.*

JOSE: Luis, if tomorrow in the morning when you wake up, you look and see that I am dead, well, I will be dead, but you can still labor. The boss will still pay you. You can still send money to your mother and your sister. That is your work. That is my work. As you say, we work together. You can be the donkey and that will take you far.

LUIS: I do not want to be a donkey.

JOSE: Ah. *Heh-heh!* You want to know the *way of the iguana.*

LUIS: What is that, papa? What is the way of the iguana?

JOSE: Luis, when you woke up this morning, what did you think would happen today? Where would we go?

LUIS: That… we would come here. We would work on the tile until we finished and then go home. Just as we have done.

JOSE: Yes. We have come to lay tile. But when a man is facing the morning sun, standing on his own two feet, he must decide where he will go and what he will do that day. Most days we already know. But a man can decide to change his plan. Make a new plan. Go a different way. Perhaps, he thinks, there is a better way to do the work of the heart. Maybe take a ship and go to Alaska, or *Tierra del Fuego in Argentina.* Maybe there is a better opportunity in a new land, like here in California.

LUIS: But we are already here, to lay the tile.

JOSE: Yes, but there is also the *way of the iguana.*

LUIS: What is that?

JOSE: To lie in the sun and do nothing. That is a choice as well.

LUIS: To lie in the sun?

JOSE: Yes. A man may decide that he does not need to go to Alaska or Argentina, or Glendale, California or Paraiso, Tabasco. The iguana, if he has eaten, would like only a nice flat rock to rest his belly and his fat tail, and to be warmed by the sun.

LUIS: That sound nice.

JOSE: Yes, it is nice. And when the iguana is hungry, then he moves to find a meal. Not before. But even as he is resting his fat tail, he is not thinking about the work in his heart. The only thing he wants is a nice rat to chew and a warm rock. That is all. But the iguana still makes his own choice about his day. The donkey, he stands in his pen and waits for the man to come and put baskets over his shoulders and load them with coffee beans. The donkey does not get to choose his labor.

     (Tomas enters)

LUIS: *Buenos Dias, Tomas.*

TOMAS: Luis, how are you? Jose.

JOSE: Hello, Tomas.

TOMAS: Why are you just sitting here? Has the boss not come yet? So, you just sit and smoke?

LUIS: Papa was telling me about the way of the iguana.

TOMAS: Oh! Yes! Jose, do you speak of the donkey?

JOSE:	Yes, Tomas. The donkey and the iguana. And which are you today?
TOMAS:	Well it looks like you two are just sitting on warm rocks! Ha-ha!
JOSE:	Oh, no. We are waiting, resting, for the boss to come and load up our baskets, with coffee beans.
TOMAS:	Or stones and mud bricks.
JOSE:	Ha! Yes, that too. Tomas, are you well, my friend? How is your wife?
TOMAS:	You know, my friend. She is beautiful but she is stupid. I should not have married her. But I wake up in the night and think how lucky I am to have this beautiful woman in my arms. But she is stupid. She thinks only of the people on the soap operas and the price of beans today.
JOSE:	Yes. My wife too. She makes tamales in Tabasco. She does not read. She just gossips with the women of the village. But she makes the tamales for my daughter to sell in her stand. She is smart, my daughter, Pia. She makes me so proud!
LUIS:	(annoyed) And me? What am I?
TOMAS:	Are you an iguana, Luis?
LUIS:	No, I am not an iguana. And I am not a donkey! I am a man. I don't want to work my whole life hauling grout and plaster.
TOMAS:	Then you must understand the story, more deeply understand. Isn't that right, Jose?
JOSE:	Son, the question of the iguana is to consider if he is free, or even aware of his freedom. But this is just a story of animals to think about truth and life.
LUIS:	I do not understand.
JOSE:	Tomas, maybe you can help him.
TOMAS:	Luis, think of the iguana, on a rock, a flat rock.
LUIS:	Yes.
TOMAS:	Think of the iguana. But think, this is not an iguana. He does not think of himself as *an iguana*. He thinks I am *me*. To him, he is himself. Do you see?
LUIS:	No, sir.
TOMAS:	You say, I am not a donkey, or I am not an iguana. But are you a man? Are any of us? I do not wake up and think *I am human*. I think, *I am me*. You are you.
LUIS:	Yes, sir.

TOMAS:	But who are you? Who will you be?
LUIS:	I don't know, sir.
TOMAS:	That is true. But think, you are the son of Jose. That is true. Jose is my friend. That is true, for now. But who are you, yourself? Do you work hard, read books, learn about the world?
LUIS:	What do you mean?
JOSE:	Son, the iguana only eats for himself and suns himself on the rock. Are you better than that?
LUIS:	Why do you ask me this? Every day I come and work with you.
TOMAS:	But Luis, you must also look into your heart and see what is there.
LUIS:	That does not make any sense. Are we going to lay tile today, or not?
TOMAS:	Look at the man! Take charge. Yes, let us lay the tile.
JOSE:	Yes, son. Pick up a bag. We will begin.

Scene 2: Paraiso, Tabasco, Mexico

> (on a main street with a row of beat up shops, a *tortilleria* has a garage-door open, and a small shop is inside. At the back, Mother tends a corn grinding machine while she is making tortillas. Pia, the daughter runs the shop.)

PIA: (walking to the back to check on Mother)

Mama. Mama?

MOTHER: Yes, Pia?

> (switches off noisy grinding machine)

PIA: (She is probably 21 or 22. Pretty. Stylish. Capable.)

Mama, you should go home. Lie down for a while. We have enough today.

MOTHER: You know I see the doctor tomorrow. I want you to have enough.

PIA: It is enough, *mami*. Go rest.

MOTHER: I am fine, Pia.

PIA: (she pulls up a stool and sits next to the woman)

I hate to send you away, to rest, when you look so happy making tortillas. But you should rest. This heat is no good for you.

MOTHER: I will rest when I am in heaven, bless *Jesus*.

PIA: Mami, don't talk like that. I don't like it when you talk like that. About being dead and in heaven.

> (teasing her – exaggerating, dramatically)

What if, mama, God sees into your heart, and sees all of your sins and all of your wickedness! All of your life of cruelty will be repaid – with the *whip of Satan!*

MOTHER: OOOHHH!! Pia! Do not say that. *Ha-ha!* You silly girl.

PIA: I am sure that the red-masked devil has a special place, in the fiery underworld, for women who have piled up so much immorality and a life of scandal, so much scaring of children. You should weep for your sins, mama!

MOTHER: *Hee-hee-hee!*

PIA: It will be like when Cortez came to Mexico and the Spaniards killed the men and raped the women. But some women did not resist, did you mama? You *welcomed* the *conquistadors!* A line of flesh-starved men, with spears, would have been standing outside your door to get at you.

MOTHER: It was war time, dear one.

PIA: Ha-ha! You are the devil-one, tiny woman.

MOTHER: Oh, yes. My days of darkness. Oh well. Are you sure you have enough for tomorrow?

PIA: Yes, mama.

MOTHER: OK. (wipes her hand, folds her apron)

PIA: Mama, what will the doctor say tomorrow?

MOTHER: He will say that I am healthy like a donkey and should go back to work.

PIA: No, mama. Please, what will he say?

MOTHER: He will poke and prod, and say, *there is nothing more to do, Señora.*

PIA: But we can go to the hospital. We could see papa in California.

MOTHER: I am old. When a woman is worn out, from working, from babies, from life, that is what happens. I will live, until one day I do not wake up. That will be that.

PIA: But mama…

MOTHER: Listen to me, Pia. You are my joy. You and Luis. I love you so much. I am so proud of you. I am a simple woman who grinds corn and makes tortillas. But you have done so much. You went from our stand beside the road, to this store. You put a roof over my head, Pia. Do not think that is a small thing. And when I am gone, you will find another poor, old woman to make tortillas for you, there are so many, and you will go on and on. You make me so happy, Pia.

PIA: Mama.

MOTHER: I wish Jose were here to see you. He has been gone with Luis so long. I worry about him, Luis. He is so young, to have to travel and hide, and work so much. I hope he does not learn the cruelty of the world.

PIA: He is a good boy. He will stay with papa.

MOTHER: Luis has a mind like Jose. He wants to think, and work. So many of the men here lay around in the park. They drink beer and do not work, do not help their families. I know many women who say their husbands, who they once loved, come home and beat them. They take the money she has earned, and he beats her. Many are raped, again and again, by their drunken husbands. The state should make beer against the law.

PIA: Why do they stay?

MOTHER: Where can they go? Back to their father's house? He is dead and she is over fifty.

PIA: Mama, why did you not go with him, to California?

MOTHER: What am I going to do in America? I do not speak the English. I only know how to make tortillas.

PIA: Maybe they need your tortillas in America.

MOTHER: Ha! Maybe. I have heard that the tortillas in America are hard and dry, and they break apart in your hands. A friend showed me on her phone a video from a *taqueria* in Baltimore where they push the meat out of a big hose, right into a stale *tortilla*. It was called Taqueria Bella. Huh! Not so pretty as my tortillas and your tamales!

PIA: They just don't know, mama. They don't know what real food is in America. You should go. You should show them.

MOTHER: No, Pia. You should go. You should show them.

PIA: I cannot leave you, mama.

MOTHER: Maybe we see what the doctor says. Maybe you should go and set up a restaurant in Nogales or El Paso. The people will come from across the border to find your tamales, dear one. You can bring Luis to make tortillas for you. He is a good boy.

PIA: No one can make tortillas like you though. No one will come across the river to get tortillas if they are not your tortillas. Yours are the best. How could we make tortillas if you are not there?

MOTHER: Tortillas are a simple thing. So simple that a peasant woman like me can make tortillas my whole life. You should go to Arizona. Texas. Go to America. There is so little here that I do not want you to stay. You have learned how to build a business. You have learned how to make money. You should go. There is only poverty here.

PIA: Thank you, mama. Maybe I will go when I hear from Luis and papa.

Scene 3: Six years have passed. Mexico.

(Morning in a cheap apartment above a garage, sparsely furnished with a mattress on the floor.)

(Luis and Marta are sprawled on the bed, tangled in sheets.)

MARTA: Eh. A cigarette.

LUIS: I am asleep. I am dreaming.

MARTA: Give me a cigarette and you can tell me your dream.

LUIS: (picks up the pack from the floor, hands it to Marta. She fishes a lighter from the sheets.)

MARTA: (she lights a cigarette, blows the smoke out grandly)

           What are you dreaming of, Luis?

LUIS: (pretending to sleep) I am dreaming that I am with a woman.

MARTA: You are with a woman.

LUIS: No, a beautiful woman.

MARTA: You dog!

LUIS: We are in a beautiful room. She wears nothing but a towel around her wet hair.

MARTA: And does she love you, this woman?

LUIS: She is only a dream. And I am here with you.

MARTA: Do you love me, Luis?

LUIS: No.

       (pause)

           Give me your smoke.

(He takes her cigarette, takes a long pull, then gives it back to her)

MARTA: Why are you here, Luis?

LUIS: To fill your belly.

MARTA: You are a pig. The last man who came here with me was a prince. He loved me madly. But he wanted to do terrible things to me. And then he was gone.

LUIS: And now you want me to do terrible things to you?

MARTA: Yes.

LUIS: No, Marta. I will torture you in my own way, by denying you the satisfaction of your pain.

MARTA: Do whatever you want to me. I am your slave.

LUIS: You are a lazy slave.

MARTA: You are a cruel master! I will jump on you like a spider and bite your neck!

LUIS: Did you read that in a book? You do not even jump out of *bed* until noon.

MARTA: I jump when I am hungry.

        (pause)

        Give me some money.

LUIS: No.

MARTA: I will beat you.

LUIS: Ha! And I will be beaten like a donkey? No, I will not give you money.

MARTA: Why do you come here? Why do you come in the middle of the night, take me like a Congo ape, and bend me and bruise me? I have marks all over my body when I am with you.

LUIS: Those are only your tattoos. I put my fingertips softly upon you.

MARTA: Please. Tell me you love me. Tell me that you find me beautiful.

LUIS: You are a painted hermit, hiding in your cave. You are a smelly animal with your fur matted and greasy. You show your bottom to the sky, but you are lucky that you do not get a bolt of lightning that would set your teeth on fire.

MARTA: Why do you abuse me, Luis? I love you.

LUIS: You love only yourself. And you love to hear me say that you are dirty. You want me to say that you have the power over me to make me turn my face away, in shame.

MARTA: Ha-ha! You are my cruel master! Kiss me!

LUIS: I will not kiss the iguana. Your face is rough and covered in poison spikes. You lie with your belly on the cool sheets, with your dirty feet and fat bottom stinking in the sun.

MARTA: My bottom is not fat!

LUIS: (he takes her cigarette again, takes a puff and gives it back)

        Marta, you lure me to your foul den and chew on me like a rat in your lizard mouth. You fill your belly with me and then rest until it is time to swallow me again. I am your prisoner.

MARTA: You are my pet.

LUIS: I am not your donkey. I must stand on my feet and face the sun.

  (He gets out of bed, puts on shirt and trousers. Looking out the window)

    Perhaps today I will go to Alaska, or Argentina.

MARTA: Stay with me, Luis. Make me a cup of tea.

LUIS: You are a lazy slave. Make me a cup of coffee.

MARTA: (gets out of bed, pulls on a robe and goes to a counter to make coffee)

LUIS: When I was in California, I worked for my father. He was a builder and I helped him. One morning he did not wake up. He was dead and I knew I was alone. But I went and told the boss that Jose would not be there that day. He found another man and we continued the labor. When the job was done that day, I took a roll of plastic and a carpet and I rolled up my father's body to bring him home, to be buried in Mexico. I drove a thousand miles or two thousand, I don't know. But when I got to Tabasco my mother was very sick.

MARTA: That's so sad. Your poor mother.

  (hands him a cup of coffee)

LUIS: I told her that her husband, Jose, was dead. She cried and told me that I should find her son, Luis. She did not recognize me. My sister had left already. She left my mother to die in peace. And soon she died, but there was no peace.

MARTA: Why not?

LUIS: This simple woman, who went to church every morning to say the Rosary for our Lady of Guadalupe, and then made tortillas behind a shop for her whole life, at the end she believed that her sins were too great even for the forgiveness of Jesus. She thought that the Lord would send her away, into the arms of the Devil, who waited for her, with chains and a spiked bit for her mouth because Satan was going to jump on her back and ride her through the gates of hell, into his dungeon of suffering, with his claws digging into the flesh of her thighs and shoulders. But, she told me, if I would bring her son to her, me, that he could take a prayer to the Blessed Virgin, saying that she would make a deal with the devil.

MARTA: What kind of deal?

LUIS: This simple woman said she would outsmart Satan by telling the Wicked One that she would spend eternity carrying the bones of the saints to the fires of Hell, so that they could be roasted. But the smoke, she knew, would go up, up into heaven, and maybe,

> maybe the angels would smell the roasting bones
> and would know, would remember that she still
> believed, in the Resurrection and the Virgin of
> Guadalupe. This tiny old woman was ready to take
> on the battle with the Devil for all eternity, because
> of her so-many sins.

MARTA: But what sins could she have?

LUIS: None. She was a saint. But... She wanted to be a martyr. She wanted to suffer, for God.

MARTA: Oh God.

LUIS: Her labor was a life of making tortillas to feed people. Her work was her devotion to heaven.

(sips the coffee)

Now kiss me, because I am going away.

MARTA: Don't go.

LUIS: I am going to Texas. My sister has written a letter. She said she went to El Paso to open a small taqueria, but she didn't have enough money, so she now makes the tortillas for another woman. She said this woman gave her a room in her house, in Texas. But this woman fell in love with my sister and wanted to be her lover. My sister refused but the woman threatened to throw her into the street. So, my sister agreed to be her lover, for a while. Then she met a man, *Ramon,* at the restaurant and he said she could live with him. She said he is nice, and kind to her and that he works hard. She said I could come and stay with them in America.

MARTA: You are leaving?

LUIS: I cannot stay here. My mother is gone. My father is dead. There is only poverty and ignorance here. I will not stay and drink beer by the fountain all day, waiting for the sun to go down and my misery to end.

MARTA: Do not go now. Wait. Stay with me.

LUIS: You are a vampire bat, sucking my blood, drinking my life. I am going.

MARTA: I think your sister is lying. There are no kind men. There is no one who is nice to me. There are no men who work hard. It is only the women who make the world, make the sun come up in the morning. Make the tortillas.

LUIS: Oh, and you will wait, here in your bed, like a fat iguana, for the rain to water your fields, to watch them sprout and grow into a bushel of lovers, with money and smiles for you? But I am already ripe, rotten, my kernels spilling into the dry stones, wasted. You have eaten me up and now I am only the naked husk. I must go, before you toss me onto the kindling, to burn me up in the fire.

MARTA: Forgive me, Luis. I am sorry I have abused you.

LUIS: Go to church, Marta. Say your prayers every day.

MARTA: Bless me, Luis, for I have sinned, against you.

LUIS: Go, and sin no more.

MARTA: But what will become of me? Why would you leave me, alone?

LUIS: You are never alone, Marta, when you have yourself. And with your fat bottom, you will not have to wait long. The lovers will knock, and bang, and pound on your door! When the men can smell that you are alone, steaming in desire, you have only to look the poor dog in the eyes, and he will follow you into any dark alley or closet.

MARTA: My bottom is not fat!

LUIS: Now, at this late hour, I have decided to go, and to seek the fortune of the cunning and the lucky

MARTA: Eh, Luis, there is more gold in wickedness.

LUIS: But I want to live my life honestly, honestly enough for heaven anyway. I must go away from your venomous tongue. Goodbye, Marta.

MARTA: Leave then, you sweating pig.

LUIS: (exits)

Scene 4: under a blazing sun in hot desert

> (Luis is alone, exhausted and near death. He kneels next to a large rock and prays.)

LUIS: Papi, I am at the end. Pray for my soul.

Mami, leave the bones of the saints for a moment and hear my words.

I loved you, mama. I am sorry we went away from you.
I loved you, papa. I am sorry that I disappointed you. I tried. I brought you back to your home. I hope that is good enough because there is nothing more, for you or for me.

I will die here in this wasteland, alone. The world had crushed me, defeated me. The *coyote* has abandoned me and I do not understand.

Did you know, how it would be for you, or for me? Did you know and we went anyway? Why? What was the point of it all? All the work, all the jobs, what have we left behind, but my bones to bleach in this sand?

The hunger and poverty of our town haunts us all, like a black ghoul who flies into the window and laughs at our suffering. And the men at the river have guns and hate us and chase us like rats. This is no world. This is no place to live. There is nowhere to be in peace. There is nothing but my suffering.

Now, here on a flat rock, I lay my head and I will rest.

(end)

Lucky One Day

by Rick Regan

November 29, 2020

<u>Characters</u>:

Kelly, mid-forties woman

Sherman, husband

Connie, Kelly's sister

Pauly, boyfriend of Connie

This is the story of Sherman and Kelly, when they win the lottery and what they do with their lives after the money comes in.

<u>Players</u>:

Kelly	Celia Gannon
Sherman	Chris Gannon
Connie	JC Marshall
Pauly	Ed Backes

Scene 1: interior of an apartment. Kelly is home from work, reading her phone

(Kelly is in her mid-40s with short black hair. She is wearing a loose T-shirt and blue jeans)

(Sherman is also mid-40s. He has short dark hair and is wearing a company polo shirt and tan trousers.)

SHERMAN: (enters) Hon, good news.

KELLY: Hey, sweetie. I'm glad you are home. Did you see the latest thing about the President and the Russian hookers?

SHERMAN: No. I didn't see that. Listen, hon, good news. I got a promotion today.

KELLY: That's wonderful, dear.

SHERMAN: Allen made me lead engineer of displays.

KELLY: For the calculators?

SHERMAN: Yeah. How about that?

KELLY: Did you get a raise?

SHERMAN: Yeah. 10%. Starting next month.

KELLY: Sherman, that's great news. Dear, you know how proud I am of you. I think you are a great engineer, but I think they are wasting your talent. Head of calculator displays? That technology is forty years old by now. You went from the keypad to displays, which is great, but Sherman, you can do better than that. I think you could be doing great things, but they are holding you back.

SHERMAN: Kel, you don't understand. This is a big step up. This is a crucial role in quality control. Next step is memory and processors.

KELLY: Sherman, you are making calculators, fabulous, incredibly powerful calculators, for people that can't add.

SHERMAN: What did the scientist say when asked, what is six plus nine?

KELLY: Wait for it...

SHERMAN: Somewhere between fourteen and sixteen, but we can't be absolutely sure.

KELLY: You've told me that a thousand times. Sherman, what about that new software company across town? I bet you could get a job there, for twice what that company pays you. They are just taking advantage of how brilliant you are and keeping all the money in Japan.

SHERMAN: It's not like that. Hokkaido Electrical Products is a global player. I have lots of opportunities at HELP.

KELLY: Ok. Ok. Whatever you say. Do you want to hear about my day?

SHERMAN: Sure.

KELLY: Well, I have good news too. You remember Tonya, from Receivables?

SHERMAN: Uh, yeah. Of course. Tanya.

KELLY: Well, she and another woman, MayLyn, she works in Sorting, are going to join the tennis club so we can play together. On Wednesday nights.

SHERMAN: Hey, that's great news.

KELLY: Yeah, and, they don't know it but, I get a new member commission from the club. It's not a lot but a little extra cash always helps.

SHERMAN: (like a rapper)

Aww yeah!

Smackin' that mon-ey, mon-ey!

Kell-y, Kell-y, riding that pony,

made out o' money!

Silver Doller Kelley!

Making that money, stackin' that cash!

KELLY: (laughing) Sherman! You're funny. I'm so proud of you. I love you, hon.

SHERMAN: I love you too, sweetie.

KELLY: Hey, there is some mail for you.

SHERMAN: (picks up the mail)

Hey, one from a publisher. Another rejection, no doubt.

(reading letter)

"Dear Mr. Murphy, we are delighted to accept your book for publication. Your novel, The Kings of Dogpark Beach, shows great emotive power and a deep understanding of the human condition. We are proud to add your debut novel for next fall's publishing calendar, just in time for the holiday book season. Congratulations! Roger Toomey, Publisher, South Side Books"

KELLY: Sherman, that's wonderful! They are going to publish your book! Oh, Sherman! You're an author!

SHERMAN: Wow! I can't believe it. They are going to publish my book! First a promotion and now this.

KELLY: Fantastic!

SHERMAN: (continuing with the mail)

Here's one from Lion's Den Pictures.

(reading)

"Dear Mr. Murphy, your upcoming novel, The Kings of Dogpark Beach, has been widely discussed in the industry and we'd like to strike while the iron is hot. At Lion's Den Pictures, we believe in making films that come from the heart and Dogpark Beach has all the elements of a heartwarming, family film, which is why we would like to extend an offer to buy the rights to the story. Find enclosed a check for one hundred thousand dollars. Please have your representation be in contact as soon as possible for further negotiations. Sincerely, Hank Maroon, Executive Producer, Lion's Den Films"

KELLY: What?! Sherman, that's amazing! They are going to make a movie of your book!

SHERMAN: Wow! I can't believe it. Wait, here's one from Publishers Clearinghouse Sweepstakes.

(reading letter)

"Dear Mr. Murphy, we have received your entry for this year's Publishers Clearinghouse Sweepstakes, and we are glad to inform you that you have won the Grand Prize of ten million dollars. We will be coming to your house on the first of November to film the surprise with our crew and deliver the Big Check. Please find enclosed the actual winnings, in the amount of Ten Million US Dollars, payable to Sherman Murphy, Skokie, Illinois."

KELLY: Oh my god! Sherman, we're rich! Sherman, we're rich!

SHERMAN: Break out the Cold Duck! There's a bottle in the fridge, in the back. I can't believe it.

KELLY: Oh, Sherman! I'm so happy! We're rich!

SHERMAN: Uh, Kel? There's one more thing. I bought a lottery ticket today. You don't think…

KELLY: You? You bought a lottery ticket? You never buy the lottery.

SHERMAN: I know. I know. I say it all the time, sucker's game, but today I saw this machine and I thought, why not.

KELLY: Well turn on the TV. They are about to do the numbers.

> (she goes to the fridge and pulls out a bottle of sparkling wine, Cold Duck. She gets some tumblers. She gives the bottle to Sherman)

SHERMAN: (fishes the ticket out of his pocket)

> Let's see. How does this work? There are a bunch of numbers on here. Let me get a pen.

KELLY: Open the wine, open the wine!

SHERMAN: Not yet. Let's see how it comes out.

> (watching the woman on TV present the numbers)

> Eleven, I've got that one. Sixteen, yep. Nine, hmmm.. here it is. Nine again, hey, I have two nines. OK. Forty-one, mmmm-hmmm. Hey, Kel, so far so good. Keep 'em coming. Twenty-Two, oh my god. And the Double Doozie Number.... Thirty-Three... yep, here it is. That's all of them.

KELLY: You got them all?

SHERMAN: Yep.

KELLY: Sherman... Sherman.... You won. You won the Double Doozie Lottery. Sherman! You WON!

SHERMAN: I won. I won. I won! I-won! I-won! I-won! I-won! I-won! I-won!

KELLY: Thirty-Five Million Dollars! Sherman! Thirty-Five Million! I can't believe it! We're so rich!

SHERMAN: Ah-ha-ha-ha-ha! Kelley! Ah-ha-ha-ha-ha! Oh, Kelly!

> (opening the wine, it fizzes and splashes everywhere, he sprays it around like a World Series celebration)

> (guzzles the wine, splashing it all over his face, then pours some over Kelly's head, she tilts her head back, drinking like it is pouring out of a fountain, splashing it all over her face)

KELLY: Ooooooooohhhhhhhh!!! This is the best day ever! Sherman! Make love to me now or lose me forever!

SHERMAN: Come, my sweet enchantress! I will ravish you!

> (Kelly runs away, Sherman chasing her. They exit to the bedroom)

(end of scene)

Scene 2: one year later, interior of new apartment, 45th floor of downtown Chicago building, huge glass window overlooking Lake Michigan. Blue sky and clouds below the window.

(Sherman sitting in a big leather chair, playing a video game by himself. He is wearing a Chicago Bulls jersey and shorts, also wearing flip-flops)

SHERMAN:	Aww yeah, come to papa… that's it, nice and easy…. And… POW! That's it! Yeah!

(Kelly enters, she is wearing a UCLA cheerleader outfit, a powder blue mini-dress with gold/yellow stripes up the sides. She has long flowing blond hair, probably a wig, and high heel shoes)

KELLY:	Sherman, are you working today or just going to play video games?

SHERMAN:	Hang on. I'm pinned down.

(he wrestles game controller and focuses on the screen)

KELLY:	Listen, Connie is on her way over. We're going to the casino for the afternoon.

SHERMAN:	(looking up, abandoning the video game)

	Casino? All the way down in Gary? With your sister?

KELLY:	No, River's, out by O'Hare.

SHERMAN:	Well, take an uber. I don't want you smashing up another Benz.

KELLY:	Hey, don't forget that you were the one drag racing a motorcycle with your Rolls. Tell me again how it felt when the cops impounded your precious car on lower Wacker?

SHERMAN:	I just don't want you two lushes blowing wads of cash, drinking casino-champagne all day and then trying to drive, no, weave your way home.

KELLY:	What are you really worried about, the car or me?

SHERMAN:	I just don't want to see you get arrested. Or hit a little kid. They'd clean me out. And why are you dressed up like a cheerleader? What is that, UCLA?

KELLY:	It's the latest fashion in Hollywood. Don't you pay attention at all? On the red-carpet, everyone is dressed as a cheerleader.

SHERMAN:	What, is this Halloween?

KELLY:	It's the world of high fashion. You know, Galliano, Lacroix, Vera Wang, they all make couture cheerleader ensembles. And look at you. Are you a walk-on for the Bulls now?

SHERMAN: I just put on something comfortable. I can't believe you are going out like that.

(Doorbell rings, then Kelly's sister Connie and her boyfriend Pauly come in.)

(Connie is dressed as a USC cheerleader, in a tight white sweater with large USC letters across the chest, and short, pleated, white skirt, with bands of burgundy and gold around the hemline. Pauly is in a Blackhawks hockey jersey, cargo shorts and flip flops.)

CONNIE: Hey, Kel, I *love* the blue on you. Is that Donatella?

KELLY: Yeah, Versace. And look at you! Who are you wearing?

CONNIE: Stella McCartney, from her ready-to-wear collection. I picked it up at her studio on Michigan Ave. this morning. Don't you love it?

KELLY: Fantastic! And who is this?

CONNIE: This is Pauly. He's my date. Hee-hee!

PAULY: Your date?

CONNIE: No, we've been together for a while. I wanted to see if Sherman would go with us and make a foursome. Hello Sherman!

SHERMAN: Connie, you are a cheerleader too?

CONNIE: Of course. It's the latest.

SHERMAN: (gets up, shakes hands with Pauly)

              Hey, how are ya? I'm Sherman.

PAULY: Yeah. Pauly. Hey, this is some place. What a view! That's a million-dollar window, right there.

KELLY: Two million. One of the Cubs players had it, but he got traded so he had to sell in a hurry. We got quite a deal.

CONNY: (mocking him) So, Sherm, you're looking good. Always in good *taste*.

SHERMAN: Says the woman dressed like a teenager. I didn't know they made those sweaters in extra-large. Is that why you need a tailor, to let the waist way out?

CONNIE: Sherm, you know since you won all that money you have turned into somebody I don't like. Crude. Crass. That's what you are.

KELLY: He hasn't worked a day since he quit his job. He just sits around here playing games.

PAULY: And porn. I bet you watch a lot of porn. I would if I had a pile of dough.

CONNIE: Pauly, you already watch a ton of porn and you don't have any money.

PAULY: Purely for research purposes.

CONNIE: Sure, sure.

PAULY: Hey, Kelly, the thong you get with that outfit, is it the blue or the yellow? I gotta know. With Connie's they went with the burgundy, which I think is a nice touch. Go ahead, Connie, flash 'em your thong.

CONNIE: Hey, Pauly! Leave Kelly alone. The only panties you are going to be sniffing are mine.

PAULY: You going to sit on my face later?

CONNIE: You can smell what I ate for breakfast.

PAULY: I already know you had a mouthful of sausage so…

CONNIE: Pauly, shut up. Enough of the bone-in, porkchop talk. These are nice people.

PAULY: I'm just saying I'd like a peek under that skirt.

SHERMAN: Hey! Hey! Back off. You just walked in here and start talking about my wife like that. What's the matter with you?

PAULY: Hey, Sherman, buddy. What's the matter? What's the matter? You so much of a fag that you don't want to slide that thong aside? Which is it, blue or yellow, honey?

SHERMAN: Listen, get the fuck out of here! Both of you.

PAULY: What, are you one of those queer rich dudes? You waiting for the wife to go out for the day and then you ring up the pool boy? You play chutes-and-ladders, I bet.

KELLY: C'mon Con, let's get out of here.

CONNIE: What, Sherman, you've got work to do?

KELLY: Honey, I need some money. Can you give me ten-thousand dollars?

SHERMAN: Take it out of the cookie jar. And, yes, Connie, I do have work to do. I day-trade crypto-currencies. But you wouldn't know anything about that.

PAULY: You mean like that BitCoin stuff? You do that?

SHERMAN: I track the market momentum and move between options on futures contracts.

CONNIE: What does that mean?

KELLY: It means, he found a new way to lose money. Except it's not as much fun as playing Pai-gow Poker at the

	casino. The Sherman Murphy Corporation doesn't actually *do* anything.
SHERMAN:	I've been in the money on a bunch of contracts.
KELLY:	And losing money on more. Sherman, at this rate you are going to *invest* us right back to that horrid little apartment in Skokie.
SHERMAN:	That little apartment was good enough for you when you were working in Receivables at the steel tubing company.
KELLY:	We lived there because we had to. Now we can live where we deserve to be. Not in Skokie.
SHERMAN:	What's the matter with Skokie? My mother lives there.
CONNIE:	Sherman, when was the last time you even left this building?
SHERMAN:	Who needs to leave? The world can come to me.
PAULY:	No, Sherm, what she means is that you should come with us to the casino. Have a day out.
SHERMAN:	What are you doing? Casing the joint? Some of your associates going to rifle the place when we leave? No way. Go if you want to but I'm staying here.
CONNIE:	Kel, I don't see why you stay with this creep. You should divorce him and take him to the cleaners.
PAULY:	Yeah. She's right. And, uh, I could be single, if you need company. Or a third wheel, if you roll like that. *Heh!*
CONNIE:	No, I mean it, Kelly. You are my little sister and I know what's best for you. This lazy bum is going to blow through your whole stack and put you back in that wet cardboard box apartment in Skokie, or worse. No. Soak him and protect yourself. You don't deserve this misery.
SHERMAN:	Connie, you get out of bed on the wrong side today? You, dressed like a cheerleader, are telling my wife to divorce me? I'm right here, you know. I can hear you.
KELLY:	Sherm, I think she's right. I have to look out for myself. I need to protect my assets.
SHERMAN:	Your assets? Yours? That's my money. My book. My movie. My lottery ticket. Mine. I'll give you enough to keep you in your kooky outfits but the money is mine. The only assets you should be worried about is putting on a longer skirt so you don't catch cold.
CONNIE:	See! See! See, Kel. All he cares about is himself. That's all he's ever cared about. I don't think he's

	ever loved you. Do you even do it anymore? I don't see how you could touch him.
PAULY:	Yeah, if mister queer-boy here isn't getting the job done, hey, I'm available.
CONNIE:	You are not. You are not available. You're mine.
PAULY:	Listen, hon, I'm keeping my options open. Maybe I should consider where my talents are best used.
CONNIE:	Keep it in your pants, Pauly.
SHERMAN:	Is this why you came here today? Huh! To break up my marriage? To convince Kelly that I'm a bum. Connie, I've had enough of you. Ever since Kelly and me have been together, you've been trying to stab me in the back. But it is Kelly that you are stabbing, not me. If we divorced, there are plenty of women who want to be with a distinguished and wealthy older man. But what will happen to her? First it was the boob job. Then the plastic surgery. Look at her face, it looks like the snare drum at a KISS concert! The wrecked cars, the dumb investments. Like giving your brother the money to start a firewood business. The guy couldn't manage a Coke machine.
KELLY:	You leave Kurt out of this. We do not speak ill of the dead.
SHERMAN:	So, don't even think about it. Get that idea out of your hollow little head.
KELLY:	My what?
SHERMAN:	If you keep going to the casino, the cookie jar will be as empty as your noggin. You've never had any brains. You used to have a hot little body, but now you have to go to a doctor to tighten up all the sags and wrinkles. There is nobody who wants to marry you, no matter how much money you steal from me.
KELLY:	Fuck you, Sherman. I'm calling a lawyer when we get back.
SHERMAN:	Back from drinking and gambling at a casino? Yeah, I bet even the man-hater, women divorce lawyers will want to jump all over your case. But they will tell you the truth, that you will get nothing and end up back at the tubing factory stacking boxes.CONNIE: Don't listen to him. He's just jealous and bitter. He's trying to turn you against your best interests. I bet he'd even try to poison you, to get rid of you.
SHERMAN:	Hell, I'm the one who is going to get poisoned. She'd love to knock me off, take all the money AND collect on life insurance. But she's already got a life of ease. Why even lift a finger, get her French-manicured hands dirty with poison?

KELLY: Well, it would be a joy to be rid of you. It brightens my mind to think of a world without Sherman. No handsy-gropes. No smelly bathroom. Have decent food, not just ribs all the time.

SHERMAN: It's paleo. Keeps me trim.

KELLY: Ribs and beer? I don't think so.

PAULY: Look, people, hey! Are we going to go get our game on, or watch these two miserable people be miserable together?

CONNIE: You're right, Pauly. Come on, Kelly. Pauly's got a car downstairs. We can talk about this on the drive.

(Pauly and Connie exit)

KELLY: I'm leaving, Sherman.

SHERMAN: No, you are not. You are going to stay right here and satisfy me with a conjugal visit on this sofa.

KELLY: No, I'm going. You can't touch me anymore. You can't hurt me anymore.

SHERMAN: Hurt you? I could never hurt you.

KELLY: I'm going to get my own place. I will have the lawyers be in touch. Goodbye, Sherman.

SHERMAN: You'll be back here tonight, drunk and horny, begging for it, stripping in front of the window. But remember, naughty wives get punished.

KELLY: Fuck you, Sherman. (exits)

SHERMAN: (alone) Bitch.

(he takes up the game controller and re-starts a video game.)

That's it… Come to papa… Bang!

(end of scene)

Scene 3: interior of the high-rise apartment, the next day

(Sherman enters. He is wearing a grey polo shirt and tan pants. He goes to the window and stands looking out)

(Kelly enters. She is wearing a pale green polo shirt and tennis skirt. Her hair is back to being short and dyed black.)

(Kelly sees him. She sits at a table or counter with a cup of coffee)

KELLY:		You ok, hon?

SHERMAN:		Dammit!

KELLY:		Sherm, what's the matter?

SHERMAN:		I got an email from my publisher this morning. They are putting the book on hold.

KELLY:		Why? Did they say why?

(Sherman goes over and sits by Kelly)

SHERMAN:		He said they got a cease-and-desist letter from Troy Beckhiem's lawyer. He is saying that I plagiarized from his book. I never even read his damn book. This is bullshit.

KELLY:		Troy? Troy that lived downstairs in Skokie? Oh, honey, I'm sorry.

SHERMAN:		On top of that, now the movie deal is on hold because of this. They "can't proceed" because of the risk of more lawsuits. Jee-suss, what an ass that guy is!

KELLY:		But look, Sherm, you don't need the book and the movie. We've got plenty of money. You should write another book. Tell your publisher you are working on a new one.

SHERMAN:		It's not about the money, Kel. It's the recognition, of my writing. Now I look like an idiot. I'm going to kill that guy.

KELLY:		Sherm, they loved your book. You worked hard on that book. Didn't you? I mean, it's not true, right?

SHERMAN:		I might have talked to him about it and swapped a few stories. He was working on his novel at the same time. Maybe I put in something he said, by accident. I don't know.

KELLY:		Oh, Sherman...

SHERMAN:		Kelly, what do you do all day? You are going to go play tennis now?

KELLY:		Well, yes. I have a lesson at one and then we start a tournament tonight, under the lights. What do you mean, what do I do all day?

SHERMAN:		I mean, what are we doing this for?

KELLY: Doing what?

SHERMAN: This, Kelly. This. You and me. Why are we still together? You never let me touch you anymore. We haven't had sex in years. Do you even like me?

KELLY: (very cold)

Sherman, you know why. After the first miscarriage… and then, having to abort because of fragile-X syndrome, I just don't want to use my body like that anymore. I know you wanted children, but I'm broken, Sherm. It doesn't work right anymore.

SHERMAN: I know. I know. You really tried. And I know it tore your heart out both times. Mine too. But I was thinking about what you said, yesterday, about a divorce. I've been really thinking.

KELLY: Don't do this. Don't do this to me.

SHERMAN: I think maybe you are right. It would be better for you to be protected from me. You deserve somebody who is kind to you. Somebody better than me.

KELLY: Sherman, no. I love you.

SHERMAN: I'll give you half. I was thinking, I'll give you half. Right now. Then, you know, we can go our own ways.

KELLY: Sherman, no.

SHERMAN: Here, look. (shows her his phone) Look, the balance in my account is about twenty-nine mil. Call it thirty. Cut in half, you get fifteen. Keep the apartment. We'll just keep that off the table. OK.

KELLY: Sherman, what are you doing? Why?

SHERMAN: OK, there. I just transferred fifteen to your account. That's yours now. You're free.

KELLY: No, Sherman. You mean you're free. You are free to leave me behind, the shrew, the bitter old crone. The nag. That's me, isn't it? You think I'm just used up and a nag.

SHERMAN: No, no. Oh, Kelly. I love you. That's why I want to do this. For your own good. I'm no good for you. But you should be happy. You can find somebody that will make you happy. Maybe one of those tennis douche-bags. I don't know.

KELLY: But I'm happy with you.

SHERMAN: No, you're not. You haven't been happy in years. I don't know why. I don't know what makes you happy anymore. Because I don't know what makes me happy. I'm not happy.

KELLY: You're not?

SHERMAN: You know me. I stare at the screen all day, getting wound up in option trading, like I'm some market wiz, but at the end of the day I'm just burned out, bitter, and down a couple, ten-thousand more. I just have to break out of this. I'm sorry. I'm the one who has to go, not you.

KELLY: Sherman, listen to me. First, I am going to keep the money. That was very generous. Thank you. Next, you can't take back what you said about me yesterday. You showed your real feelings, for once. But I look at you and I know that there is a kind, gentle man in there. Maybe he's lost or gets pushed aside by the day to day. But he's in there and I have faith in you, Sherm.

SHERMAN: I know you mean that, hon. You have been with me through the ups and downs. But you still have to answer the real question about life, what is worth doing?

KELLY: How do you, anybody, how does anybody answer that?

SHERMAN: Is playing tennis the best you can do? Is playing video games the best I can do? Investing? Huh. It's just another video game. Where I'm the loser again.

KELLY: We can make changes, can't we?

SHERMAN: It's not about changing. Well, it is about changing, but what I have to change is myself. And let you go so you can make whatever changes you need. I want to take a trip, go see the ocean.

KELLY: Sherm, we've got Lake Michigan right out the window, for Pete's sake.

SHERMAN: It's not the water, Kelly. I want to change my life. I'm sorry, but the show's over. I'm going to put a bag together and take off. I'll take the Rolls. You keep the Benz.

    (Sherman exits, into a bedroom)

KELLY: (She looks after him, then starts to cry softly)

SHERMAN: (returns with a suitcase, laptop case and a windbreaker)

I love you, hon. Make whatever arrangements you want. I'll sign the papers.

KELLY: (through tears) Oh, Sherman, why are you trying to hurt me this way? I'm not going to file for divorce. I'll just wait until you get back, until you clear your head or whatever it is that you are doing. But I don't understand. I don't understand, Sherman.

SHERMAN: Kel, you should be happy. You won't be happy with me. Find your own happiness. Do that for me.

KELLY: But where are you going?

SHERMAN: I always wanted to see New Orleans. Maybe I'll follow the river, I don't know.

KELLY: But Sherman, you are my husband. You can't just walk out on me.

SHERMAN: Yes, I can. Like you wanted to do yesterday but chickened-out. Well, I'm not chickening-out. Good bye, Kelly. Have a nice life, without me.

(Sherman goes out the door)

KELLY: (crying) Why are you doing this to me?

(yelling at the door)

Eat shit, you rancid mother-fucker! I hate you! I hope you drive your goddamn Rolls Royce into the river, and drown! I can be happy. I can be happy! I can be a hell of a lot happier - without you. Goodbye, Sherman Murphy. Hello happy! Fuck you!

(gets up and stomps into the bedroom)

(she storms back out, wielding a souvenir baseball bat)

Fuck you, Sherman!

(she smashes the gaming console with the bat, bashing it angerly)

(she stops, breathing hard, staring at the smashed plastic pieces)

Fuck you, Sherman. I never loved you.

(she throws the bat at the smashed device on the floor)

(she exits.)

(end)

Smarty Marty

By Rick Regan

November 11, 2020

This is the story about a farmer in Ireland who is looking for a new horse to replace MacDougal, one of his other horses. He goes to the market to find a new horse.

Characters:

Tommy	Irish Farmer
Jimmy	Irish Farmer
Mick	Auctioneer
Marty	Talking Mule

Characters:

Tommy	Ed Backes
Jimmy	Chris Gannon
Mick/Auction	JC Marshall
Marty	Celia Gannon

SCENE ONE.

FARMER TOM'S barn, rural Ireland, present day, morning.

FARMER TOM opens the door, sees his horse MacGuire but the stall next to the horse is empty.

TOMMY: Well, MacGuire ol' boy. I guess it's time. You've been alone long enough I suppose. The grief has run through us both, run it's course. The fever is gone. I think it's time to head into town now and see if there is a smart-aleck horse to match you in the harness.

No big fella is going to be a match for ol' MacDougal, bless him, but maybe there will be one with a sense of humor for you, you mischievous rascal. When they say down at the pool that there should be no rough horse-play, be-god I know the meaning of it.

Why, reminds me of the time, years ago, ya'know, there was the two of ya' in the turf, hitched up side-beside, and weren't the two of ye' devils throwin' peat at each other, sideways like. Christ, the scrubbin' it took that day to clean youse two up. Heh. Yeah, old MacDougal, I'll miss him for sure. A good horse, him.

Well and away I'll go then. I'll be back in a couple of hours time.

(exits)

SCENE 2 MORNING AT THE MARKET IN COROFIN, IRELAND

(The market has vegetable sellers with potatoes, carrots, etc. There are cheese , milk and egg sellers, and fresh flower vendors. At the end there is a stable with various horses and animals for sale..)

(Above one stall is a sign, "Mule for Sale, Best Offer")

(The mule in the stall has a sign around his neck that says, "I am Marty. I am a bad mule.")

TOMMY: (looks at the horses, then sees the mule sign)
Well now, what is your crime, Mister Marty? Did you trample the veg in the garden or eat all the lettuces to the nubs? Heh! A bad mule.

JIMMY: (enters, sees his friend Farmer TOM)

TOMMY: Jimmy-boy- o, if it isn't yerself. Why it would be near on a year I've seen ya'. Where have ye been keepin' yerself then?

TOMMY: Ah, Jimmy. It is true a light in my day, to see you , sir. You're lookin' well. Have ye' been after the barman for the tomato juice, instead of the *black stuff*?

JIMMY: Tommy, ah-surely I haven't seen you in an age. Have ye' been alright then?

TOMMY: (glum) Well, ye' know, perhaps ye' heard, it was my old boy MacDougal, went down last November. He was a good horse but he was a trouble maker.

JIMMY: Sure, yeah, I remember MacDougal. Great broad chest on that one. Fine, pretty legs for a draught'er.

TOMMY: Ah, indeed. Ye' know the very one. Well, himself and MacGuire were out on the turf field in back, just horsin' around, trying to make each other laugh, don't ye' know.

JIMMY: Heh! Like they do.

TOMMY: Well, sure now, don't I look out my kitchen window, seeing those two rascals, and they just having a right pissing contest?

JIMMY: What do ya' mean, Tommy? A pissin' contest?

TOMMY: Sure and aren't they both measuring out, in steps, which o' them two can piss the furthest.

JIMMY: I'll be damned! Horses?

TOMMY: Right!

JIMMY: Ah, well, can't come down too hard. Been at it myself, down the pub.

TOMMY: Ya' suppose it's just in the male nature, like a character thing?

JIMMY: Could be, Tommy, could be. But, tell me, which one was the winner?

TOMMY: Ah, Jimmy, there I am having a right laugh at these two, when MacDougal hits the wire on the electric fence. The volts go right up the stream, straight through his willie and stops his heart. He jumped a great mile, straight up, then fell to the ground like a sack of coal. Never took another breath.

JIMMY: Christ on the Cross, Tommy! That's a terrible thing to happen to a good horse.

TOMMY: Well, I chalk it up to him getting what he deserved from his devilment. And he was getting up the years, you know, so it would have been that, or something else.

JIMMY: Still, it is a hard thing to lose a friend as true as MacDougal. So you've been consoling yourself with the poteen then? It's a powerful remedy but it does not lift the heart.

TOMMY: It does not, as you say Jimmy, lift the heart. I've had to put down the drink, six months now, just to get out of bed in the morning. But, and this is the tough patch, the whole thing has been even harder on MacGuire, what with him seeing his best pal drop dead in the field, and the stall next to him quiet and dusty.

JIMMY: Ah, sure, the poor devil. Loneliness is rough on a smart horse.

TOMMY: It is, Jimmy. It is indeed.

JIMMY: So have ye' come to town to sight a new pal for your MacGuire, is it?

TOMMY: It is, Jimmy. It is indeed.

JIMMY: Ah well, steer clear of this fella. He's not worth the feed I give him.
           (points a thumb at the mule, Marty)

TOMMY: Why, sure, this is your mule, is it not?

JIMMY: It is, Tommy. It is indeed.

TOMMY: What's his crime, that you've got him for sale? You raised him from a foal. Why ya' doin' this, Jimmy?

JIMMY: Ah, Tommy, I've outsmarted me-ownself, ya' see.

TOMMY: Have ya' now?

JIMMY: Aye. Ye' see, Tommy, I'd gotten a book, from the Internet, ya' know, on how to teach a mule to speak.

TOMMY: Ye' didn't?!

JIMMY: Aye.

TOMMY: And now ye' feel the fool, for spending the money, on the Internet? For you can't teach a mule to speak, now can ye'?

JIMMY: Well, ye' wouldn't believe me if I told ye', but sure as the sun comes up, this mule learned to talk. Now he's driving me daft. I can't take it, is all.

TOMMY: Why that sounds like a grand thing, Jimmy. Teaching a mule to talk? Amazing!

JIMMY: No, it is not, Tommy. It certainly is not. Ye' see, I wanted to understand the working of the animal mind. To hear, in his own words, the experience of the mule. But what he's got is a head full of rubbish. First, all he talked about was how hungry he was, so I fed him and then fed him some more. But soon I realized he was having me on. And by the hair-on-my-head, wasn't he getting just as wide as he was long.

TOMMY: Playing you the fool, Jimmy? The useful idiot?

JIMMY: Indeed he was, Tommy. But that's not the thing that's got him in this pickle now. It certainly is not.

TOMMY: Oh, what's that then?

JIMMY: Sure, didn't Marty get himself into a box of old film magazines, about celebrities and the like.

TOMMY: No! The devil.

JIMMY: And now he's obsessed with the great ones of the silver screen from the early-two-thousands.

TOMMY: Is he?

JIMMY: Aye. Scarlett Johansson, ye' know. Helena Bonham Carter, it is. Kate Blan-chette, even!

TOMMY: (laughs) Jesus, Jimmy, you're havin' me one. Sure, this whole thing, talking mule. And didn't I just believe you? Ah you're swell, Jimmy. Heh!

JIMMY: No! It's true. It's all he goes on about! Driving me mad. I told him, he damned-well better behave himself here so that he can be a pox on some other poor soul.

TOMMY: Aww now, Jimmy. Yer' pulling myleg. He's right here. If he can talk, why don't ye show me?

JIMMY: Ah, once ye' get him started, he won't shut up...

TOMMY: Ah, you're lying, Jimmy. Go on with ya'.

JIMMY: Well, Tommy, all I will say is that you can take the blame yourself. Alright, Marty!
(yells at the mule)

	Marty! Wake up, now. What's on yer' demented mind this morning, Marty?
MARTY	Can I get a hot dog? You got a hot dog?
	(to Tommy) Can you get me a hot dog? Foot long, schmeer of mustard, lots of relish. Lots of relish.
TOMMY:	Christ! I can't be-lieve it. A talking mule!
MARTY	C'mon. You got thumbs. Get me a hot dog. I like hot dogs.
JIMMY:	(exasperated) Ah, here we go with the hot dogs...
MARTY	Hey, is that Helena Bonham Carter over there?

(both men turn around)
Ha! Made you look!

| JIMMY: | Oh, devil in heaven... |
| MARTY | Is that Kate Blanchette? She could saddle me up all day. I'd ride her around all night. |

(Jimmy puts his hand to his forehead)
Can you put Scarlette Johannson in the stall next to me? I swear I won't peak when you are washing and brushing her. I swear. OK, I'd look. You can hitch her to the cider press with me and I'd walk around in circles all day. Maybe not Winona Rider though. She looks like she smells bad.

TOMMY:	What is this?
JIMMY:	I told you. He got into a box of tabloid magazines. I get them from the news agent in town when they are expired, and he's going to throw them out. I put them through the shredder and spread them in the barn in winter. But he chewed a box open and flips the pages with his tongue. He's obsessed!
MARTY	I want to plow a field with Maggie Gyllenhaal. She's got nice ears. She could nibble on my ears. I would look at her ears when we are hitched up in the side-by-side. She has nice ears. I wonder what she smells like. Probably like fresh cut grass. Or barley. Mmmm...
TOMMY:	I see the trouble you've got here, Jimmy.
JIMMY:	I blame myself, and myself alone. Had I not worked to teach this beast to speak, all would be well. It is myself alone to blame.
TOMMY:	Ah, cheer up, Jimmy. There will be a buyer along soon. And you'll be rid of him.
AUCTION	(enters, sees Tommy and Jimmy) And who have we got here? Jimmy, it is yourself. And ol' Tom, you're a hard fella, ain't ya?
TOMMY:	Mick, what is it for you today? Why the special hat?

AUCTION	(takes off hat that says "Special") Sure, look, Tom. It's a Special Hat. I'm an auctioneer, you know.
TOMMY:	Ye' don't say! Auctioneer? How's that work, then?
AUCTION	(puts hat back on, pulls out notepad and pencil) Well, like this, then. This mule here, for sale, what would you give for him?
TOMMY:	Well, I don't know, like. Maybe, a Euro note.
JIMMY:	It's a talking mule, Tommy! Worth more than that, sure.
AUCTION	One Euro, one Euro. I have one Euro. Can I get two? Two Euro, two Euro..
TOMMY:	I suppose I could see two..
AUCTION	I have two Euro, two Euro. Can I get five? Five Euro, five Euro...
JIMMY:	But he can talk, Tom.
TOMMY:	Well, all right, five then.
AUCTION	Five Euro, five Euro. Do I hear ten? Do I hear ten? Ten, ten, ten, ten. Ten Euro.
JIMMY:	I trained him myself, Tom.
TOMMY:	Maybe ten.
AUCTION	Ten! Ten, ten, ten. Is there twenty-five? Twenty-five, twenty-five. Can I get twenty five?
JIMMY:	You've got MacGuire all alone at home, Tom. Think of the horse for a moment.
TOMMY:	I suppose twenty five is not too much for a friend for Macguire.
AUCTION	Twenty! Five! Twenty-five! Do I hear One HUNdred? One Hundred? One Hundred for the talking mule? A mule that talks folks!
TOMMY:	Jesus, no!
AUCTION	Is there Fifty? Fifty! Is there fifty, for the talking mule? Fifty!
JIMMY:	But he talks, Tom. Maybe he can teach the other horse to talk.
TOMMY:	Hmmm. Maybe. Ok. Fifty.
AUCTION	FIFTY! We have fifty! Can we have one HUNdred? One HUNdred! One HUNdred!
TOMMY:	Full stop, no. Fifty, and that's it, Jimmy.
JIMMY:	But he can talk. I taught him myself.

TOMMY: Full stop. I'll give you fifty.

AUCTION   Fifty! Fifty. Going once! Fifty! Going twice! Fifty!
                Fifty! Fifty Euro... SOLD! Fifty Euro for the talking
                mule.

        (slaps his note pad like a auction gavel)

JIMMY: Well done, Mick!

        (shakes hands with the Auctioneer)

TOMMY: (gives Jimmy Fifty Euros)
                Well, I'll take him back and see if MacGuire can
                make some sense with him. Do youse know anybody
                who'd be into making a film like, of a talking mule?

AUCTION   I've got a cousin, you know, who does such things in
                Cork. I'll put him on to ya', Tom.

TOMMY: T'anks Mick.

AUCTION   Good day to you, gentlemen.

        (Auctioneer leaves, tips his hat)

TOMMY: (hitches up Marty, leads him out of stall)
                Well, Jimmy, I'll be seeing you. Thanks for the mule.

JIMMY: But Tommy? Why did you get the mule? He's a right
                ass.

TOMMY: Well, Jimmy, my thinking is this, if he can learn to
                speak, and read about film stars, then maybe I'll feed
                him some financial magazines. Maybe he'll have an
                eye for the undiscovered growth-stock like, or sports
                teams that might be a solid punt. But really, Jimmy,
                I'm thinking of the You-Tube.

JIMMY: The You-Tube?

TOMMY: Right. If I feed him some news papers or political
                type things, maybe wit' a Go-Pro, I could make a few
                of them memes, ya' know, on the You -Tube. That
                would be cracking good fun, wouldn't it Jimmy. A
                mule that says the strangest things about the
                councilor up the road, or the prime minister. I
                suppose the real money is in the American Market
                though, saying silly stuff about the President. That
                would be sound.

JIMMY: You're on to something there. I like it. I'll adjust my
                settings for the You-Tube channel and watch for ya.

TOMMY: Well, we've got work to do so I'll be off then, Thanks
                again, Jimmy
                (walking out with MARTY)

MARTY   Where are we going? We going for hot dogs?

TOMMY: To the Kate Wins-lette's house, Marty.

MARTY Oh, Kate Wins-lette! I like her ears. She's got nice ears. I'll nibble her ears all night.

TOMMY: Sure, you will, Marty. Sure you will. And the Mi-chelle Pfeiffer too. Sure.

MARTY Oh boy! The Mi-chelle Pfeiffer too, ya' say? Oh boy! I like her. She could ride me all day. All day.

(exit)

END

9 798564 560931